# HOOP CITY

## NEW YORK CITY

### SAM MOUSSAVI

EPIC
Press

# New York City
## Hoop City: Book #4

Written by Sam Moussavi

Copyright © 2016 by Abdo Consulting Group, Inc.

Published by EPIC Press™
PO Box 398166
Minneapolis, MN 55439

Cover design by Nicole Ramsay
Images for cover art obtained from Shutterstock.com
Edited by Lisa Owens

LIBRARY OF CONGRESS CATALOGING-IN-PUBLICATION DATA

Moussavi, Sam.
New York City / Sam Moussavi.
p. cm. — (Hoop city)
Summary: Darnell is a talented high school basketball player from Brooklyn, primed
to be the first to attend college in his family. When his mother tells him that she
has a new boyfriend, an event from Darnell's past takes him to a dark place that will
force him to confront it.
ISBN 978-1-68076-047-7 (hardcover)
1. Basketball—Fiction. 2. High schools—Fiction. 3. Inner cities—Fiction.
4. Teamwork—Fiction. 5. Young adult fiction. I. Title.
[Fic]—dc23
2015903977

EPIC
Press

EPICPRESS.COM

*To Marina, with a white butterfly fluttering just above her shoulder*

# ONE

"Darnell," she said. "Darnell."

I blinked a couple of times and saw that it was still dark outside. I could still hear the cars through my window, though, filled with folks trying to get to work and school.

"Boy," she said with a little more force, "I'm not gonna tell you again."

She flicked on the light and that did it. I was out of my sleep and back into the world.

"You were late to school yesterday," she said. "School called me and said so."

My mother was a hard woman. She didn't look it because of her small size, but she was.

"I have to get to work," she said with a cup of something warm in her hand, "and *you* need to get your lazy ass out of bed."

My mother always worked. I couldn't remember a time when she didn't work.

"Alright," I said.

She took a sip from her cup and smiled. She left my room and went into her room to finish getting ready for work.

I shuffled around a little bit, trying to knock the sleep out of my body completely. I looked out the window and saw the first rays of sunshine peeking through the heavy morning clouds. It looked like it was going to be a chilly day. The calendar read October fifteenth; it was the first official day of basketball season.

I took a quick shower and by the time I got out, my mother was already gone. She left a note in the kitchen reminding me to have breakfast. She set out cereal and a banana, the same as every other day. The cereal used to be the sweet stuff—the stuff that was packed with sugar—when my mother didn't know any better. She knew better now, though. The cereal wasn't so sweet anymore.

I got my things together for school and hit the door with plenty of time to get there before the first bell. Flatbush Avenue was already humming and it wasn't even seven thirty yet. The legit people who did business on the avenue were busy sweeping the entrances to their establishments. The hustlers were out there, too, yawning because they either hadn't been to sleep yet or were just waking up. I nodded and shook hands with a few of the folks on both sides. Brooklyn was all I knew and these were my people. I couldn't really see my life outside of Brooklyn. There didn't seem to be any other place in the world for me.

——

I took the "L" to school in those days. School was only a few blocks away from the stop where I got off. It felt good to be early, probably because I was late so often. It's not that I didn't like school. I was an okay student and I showed up to classes. I did my work most of the time. I just hated waking up in the morning.

My mother was the opposite; she seemed to love the mornings. I didn't understand it. She would always tell me that not getting up in the morning is the mark of a lazy man, and that a lazy man scares people. People don't want to give a lazy man a job, she would tell me. People don't want to help a lazy man out.

There were a few girls outside of my first class and they all blushed—as much as black girls could blush—when they saw me. I gave them all a little smile before entering the classroom. It felt good to be loved at school, even though ninety-nine percent of the people there knew nothing about me other than the fact that I could play ball. I didn't care, though. The attention felt good—especially the attention from girls. That was another conversation my mother had with me a lot. And I mean a lot.

"Yo, D," someone whispered from the desk behind me.

I turned around to see that it was Yasin.

"What up, Yasin?" I said.

"Yo, Shante wanna hook up with you," he said. "She asked me to put in a good word."

"You ain't my pimp, nigga," I said with a chuckle.

"I know," he said. "I'm just saying."

"I'm good," I said. "She ain't my type."

I turned back around and the teacher was in front of the class ready to teach us about the U.S. Government.

—

Coach called me into his office during my lunch period. I swung by the cafeteria to grab a sandwich before meeting him. Coach was sitting at his desk when I came into his office. He looked up and frowned at me. I took a bite of my sandwich and my shoulders slumped a bit. He pointed to the chair in front of his desk.

"You're late," he said.

"I'm sorry, Coach," I said. "I was hungry."

"That's no excuse," he said. "You had time between class and when I asked you to meet. That's why I said twelve fifteen. Now you're gonna be late to class and I can't have that."

I didn't say anything.

"You have to be accountable," he continued. "You know the attendance office told me you already have twenty tardies for the year?"

He held up a stack of tardy slips and then slapped them back down on the desk.

"You're one of the most talented players I've ever coached, Darnell," he said. "You've even got a brain up there," he said, pointing to his head. "But you are also lazy."

There was that word again.

Coach was not one of those coaches who kissed a player's ass. He talked straight and wasn't afraid to hurt anyone's feelings. It didn't matter if you were a star player or a benchwarmer. When I was looking at high schools, or rather when high schools were looking at me to come play basketball for them, my mother ended up making the decision because of Coach. She liked that he told the truth and would be hard on me. She knew that I needed a strong male in my life on account of my father leaving when I was a baby.

"If I have one job this season," he said, "it's to motivate you."

"Okay, Coach."

"I mean it," he said. "I'm gonna be all over you this season. We have a young team and I need you to be a leader. Not just on the floor, but in the locker room too."

"I'll become a leader," I said.

"That means no more showing up late for school," he said, "no more being late for appointments."

I nodded my head. The bell rang and signaled the end of my lunch period.

"I gotta go, Coach," I said. "Fifth period."

"Get out of here," he said.

I got up from the chair and started to leave the office.

"And stay away from the girls, Darnell!" he yelled to me when I got to the doorway.

I turned around and smiled.

# TWO

I was in the trainer's room right after school to get my ankles taped. I didn't hang out with any of the girls that were waiting by my locker after the last bell. I wanted to be the first one out for practice.

To my disappointment though, another player had beat me to the punch and was already out on the court shooting free throws when I got out there.

"What's up Darnell?" Leonard said.

Leonard was our starting center and almost seven feet tall. Like me, he was a senior, and also like me, he would have his pick of just about any college in the country. I wondered if Coach had given Leonard the same "leader" speech that he'd given me, but I didn't ask.

I gave him a nod as I walked past to the far side of the gym. I leaned against the wall and kicked each of my legs out in a swinging motion. With my back to the court, I could hear the results of Leonard's free throw attempts. He took three dribbles between each shot, pausing for a half-second before releasing the ball into the air. It sounded like Leonard had worked on his free throws over the summer because he didn't miss one shot while I stretched. In fact, they were all swishes.

I finished up with my stretches and jogged the length of the court a few times. Leonard continued shooting his free throws, making every one. If the first day of the season was a sign for what was to come, we looked to be in good shape. Our star center fixed the one major weakness in his game. His free throws were so bad the previous season that Coach had to bench him toward the end of games for fear of teams fouling him intentionally. As for me, I took what Coach told me about being a leader to heart. I wanted to be better. I didn't want to just rely on my talent anymore.

Guys started coming out of the locker room in pairs, and suddenly we were a team again. This would be our first full practice together since the last one of the previous season. Even though some of us played on the same AAU squad in the summer and worked out together in the fall, there was a fresh feeling in the air.

We formed three lines across the court for stretches before the coaches even came out. Leonard, Tramon, and I—the only seniors on the team—stood at the heads of the three lines. When the coaches came onto the court, they looked out at us with approval. After we finished stretching, we jumped right into layup lines and then three-on-two drills. Coach didn't even blow a whistle or say a word during the first twenty minutes of practice.

The first whistle finally came and we all stopped to look up at Coach. He brought us up to midcourt and welcomed us to the start of the new season. He told us that the season would be long and reminded us that our schedule would be challenging. As an independent private school with no conference or sectional affiliation, we picked the teams we played against. Coach always chose the hardest opponents. He didn't believe in playing against soft teams. He finished his opening remarks by saying, "I picked this schedule because I want you guys to learn something. I want you to learn something about yourselves and I want you to learn something about life."

He blew his whistle forcefully and put us in line for our first defensive-stance drills of the season.

———

Coach didn't like to mess around in practice. He wanted us to work fast and work hard, and defense was definitely his thing. We spent more time on defense than anything else. He didn't feel the need to spend that much time on offense because Leonard and I alone could score almost as much as any other team. That actually happened in two games during our junior year.

Coach blew his whistle in short, compact bursts during the defensive drill. Each time we heard the shrill sound, we got down in our stances and stayed there until the next whistle. I could hear my teammates behind me groan each time Coach's whistle sounded. My legs were sore too, but I wouldn't show any weakness. The rest of the guys weren't going to see me relax.

The first and only break came, and the guys ran straight to the sideline to get some air and Gatorade. I went over to Coach instead. His whistle was still resting in his mouth, and he looked like he took pleasure in making us sweat. He let the whistle drop when I approached.

"Nice start," he said.

"Let me know what you need from me, Coach," I said.

He smiled. "Go get some water, hot-shot."

We started up again and it was time for the best part of practice. Any player will tell you that practice isn't much fun; most drills are boring. Working on defense feels like a chore, but we endured it all to get to the scrimmage. That's what it's all about—those last twenty to thirty minutes of practice when you can just let it all go.

Coach split the teams up evenly, meaning he put Leonard on one team and me on the other. He told us that the scrimmage would be just like a game. The only restriction was that each side had to pass the ball at least five times on each offensive possession. If we scored on a possession without passing it five times, the bucket would not count.

The first offensive possession was awkward for the other side. They couldn't manage to pass the ball five times before attacking the basket. With that knowledge, we made it really hard for them to find passing lanes. After I almost stole a pass, Terrance—a sophomore on my side—knocked a pass down, took possession, and quickly passed it to me. Even though point guard wasn't my natural position, I handled the ball a lot. I brought the ball up the court and looked for the first safe pass I could find. I knew I had to look to my teammates more often—not only because of Coach's rule in the scrimmage, but because it was the right way to play the game.

I passed to the wing and he shot it right back to me. Counting Terrance's pass to me after his steal, we had three passes. I quickly moved the ball to the opposite wing and he gave me a pass right back. That was four. With one more to go, I scanned the perimeter looking for a safe pass and saw Terrance flash and cut backdoor. I threw him a high lob along the baseline—so high that it went over Leonard's outstretched arm—and Terrance rose up and slammed it down with two hands.

Five passes. The score was two-nothing, our way.

The other side's next five possessions went mostly like the first one. They seemed lost as they kept trying to force the ball down into Leonard, either failing to realize or forgetting that he couldn't attack the basket until the fifth pass had been completed.

I had a couple more steals on defense and three more assists on the offensive end. When my team was on offense, the other side was so worried about me attacking the rim after the fifth pass that they would leave huge lanes open for the rest of my guys. I didn't even take a shot—not a single shot—during the first fifteen minutes of the scrimmage. That was unheard of for me, but I didn't need to shoot. We were up twenty to five after the first fifteen minutes.

In a strange way, Coach's restriction on the scrimmage gave me even more freedom. With the ball in my hands, I felt like I could control the entire floor and send the other nine players in any direction that I pleased. I liked *that* feeling. I wasn't sure if I could keep it up for an entire season, let alone a few games, because dominating the game without having to score was new to me.

I was always the main scorer on my team. Scoring came easy to me. But this new style of passing the ball because I wanted to instead of just passing when I was in trouble was exciting. I wanted to see if I could succeed like that. I wanted to see if *we* could succeed like that.

When the scrimmage ended, my side was ahead by twenty points. I never took a shot, but made so many assists that I lost count. Coach called us to midcourt after the buzzer sounded and we circled up around him. He looked around the circle.

"That's what it's gonna take."

He looked to his assistant coaches standing on the outer edges of the circle.

They shook their heads in agreement.

"Okay, guys," he said. "Get home safe. Put

some good food in your body. Do your home-work. Give your body plenty of rest. Be ready to do it all again tomorrow."

# THREE

"Hey, what's happening, young blood?" said an older, scratchy voice from behind.

I turned around to see what looked to be a homeless person.

"Nah," I said. "No change. Sorry."

The trains were usually late at that hour and the platforms were packed with people. I looked around to see the usual crowd: white men in suits standing next to thin, white women in dresses; hipsters on their way to the bars and restaurants; construction guys and other working-class folk. Even though we looked different, we were all in the same boat waiting for that train to come.

I was tired. It always hit me when I got to the station and waited for the train. I felt a buzz immediately after every practice that was almost like heaven. I felt like I could get back out on the court and keep running—like I could run all damn night. But when my body cooled down and the buzz wore off, I was just as tired as the construction worker.

I pulled my headphones out of my backpack and connected them to my phone. I put on some music and closed my eyes. When the train arrived, we made room for the folks getting off the train to pass before anxiously piling in. I managed to grab a seat and closed my eyes again, letting the beat of the music combined with the clanging of the subway tracks take me to the quiet place in my mind that exists right before sleep. I knew I had somewhere around fifteen minutes before arriving at my stop, and that was enough time for a little nap.

The subway was a perfect place to shut down my thoughts. There was something magical about it, actually. I didn't have any responsibility in those tunnels. Up above on the streets of Brooklyn, I had to be strong—strong for my teammates, strong for my mother. Underground, I was able to just sit in my seat—if there was one to be had—and close my eyes.

My eyes opened right before my stop and I exited the train smoothly. It was already eight o'clock when my feet hit the sidewalk. I saw a few people I knew walking through my neighborhood, but I was too tired to chop it up. I just left my headphones in and gave a nod here and there.

I walked into my apartment around eight fifteen and my mother wasn't home. That was odd, but not too odd. She worked late all the time, but usually she'd let me know first.

I dropped my bags and headed straight for the kitchen. As hard as my mother worked, there was always home-cooked food for dinner. Even when she wasn't home to serve it, all I had to do was look inside the refrigerator. Most of my teammates were on scholarship like me, but none of them ate like me. The food they ate came out of paper boxes, plastic wrappers, and to-go containers. I found none of that when I looked inside my refrigerator. I was lucky to have my mother.

I made myself a plate of grilled chicken with asparagus and roasted potatoes, and warmed it up in the oven. The smell made my mouth water. Instead of waiting until it was heated through, I took it out of oven and devoured it half-cold. It was delicious all the same.

After cleaning up, I took a shower. It was nine thirty by the time I got out, and my mother was still not home. I called her cell and she didn't pick up. I sent her a text asking where she was and she didn't reply. It was just some big thing going on at work, I thought. She was a secretary in a law firm downtown—one of the fancy ones with a long-ass name—and she and the lawyers were most likely buried in documents for the next big case.

I tried to do my homework, but couldn't focus. I was too tired. I sat on the couch and watched a little TV before falling asleep. It was eleven o'clock when the music from *SportsCenter* woke me up. She still wasn't home. I checked my phone and saw that she had called and sent me a text message, which read, *Workin' late. Hope u had a good practice. B home soon :)* She'd sent the text at ten fifty.

I went to my room and got into bed. I wanted to wait up for her, but as soon as my head hit the pillow, my eyes closed.

At some point soon after, I heard the front door open and close. I heard her soft footsteps throughout the apartment, and I heard her stop in front of my room. She opened my door and peaked inside. I was too tired to get out of bed or even say a word. I only had energy to lazily clap my eyes open and shut until they closed for good.

I could sleep comfortably knowing that she was home. She could sleep comfortably too, knowing I was safe and in bed.

———

My mother and I sat across from each other at the kitchen table the next morning.

"Work is crazy right now, huh?" I asked after a sip of orange juice.

She looked rested even though she only had a few hours of sleep.

"Yeah, there's a lot going on right now," she said after a sip of coffee.

"Practice was hard yesterday," I said. "We worked on defense for like, the whole time."

She just smiled.

"Darnell," she said. "Let's meet for dinner after practice tonight. The diner on a hundred and thirtieth."

"Okay."

"It's been a long time since we've been out together," she said.

"It's a date," I said.

"Seven thirty?" she asked.

"Can't wait," I said.

———

I got to school early that morning. That made two days in row. If I could just get all of my homework done, then I'd really be on point.

I walked to my locker and opened it. I took a few of the books that I'd need and dropped off a couple that I wouldn't. There were footsteps coming toward me, but I couldn't see who they belonged to because my head was in my locker. The person was wearing strong perfume though, so I knew it was a girl.

When I closed the door to my locker, her face was right behind it, smiling. It was Jessica, a rich white girl. We were both seniors now, but when we were sophomores, we had a lot of classes together. I knew then that she liked me. I knew it from the moment we met. But I always kept my distance from her, always saying that we were just friends.

"Hi," she said.

"What's up?"

She had green eyes and straight black hair. Her face was clean, her teeth were straight, and she had the body of a goddess. She had hips and an ass like one of the black girls from my neighborhood—a rap-video ass.

"What are you doing this weekend?" she asked.

Her perfume was strong and went straight to my head.

"Uh, I have practice and then . . . I don't know. Nothing. No plans."

"Well," she said as she pivoted on the ball of her right foot, "my folks are going out of town and I have the whole house to myself. You should come through."

I chuckled. "Yeah? And what do you have in mind?"

She leaned in and kissed me softly on the lips. Her lip-gloss was sweet and tasted of berries. She then moved to my ear and gave it a little nibble.

She pulled away and I gasped. "Come through and I'll show you," she said.

"I'll see what's up," I said, still dizzy from her perfume and all the rest of it.

"Okay," she said, then turned around and walked away.

I watched her ass as it got smaller and smaller down the hallway. It was getting harder and harder to keep her at a distance.

———

Being in class that day was a total waste of time. Jessica was the only thing I could think about, and when I wasn't thinking of her, I thought about dinner with my mother. She was right; it had been a while since we spent time together outside of the apartment. With me, it was always basketball. With her, it was always work. Neither of us had much of a life otherwise.

I was in the locker room getting ready for practice when Coach called me into his office. When I walked in, he told me sit and I did so.

"Okay, there's no use beating around the bush anymore," he said with a tone that was serious, but not one that said I was in trouble. "I'm going to name you team captain, Darnell."

I knew this was coming, but it still felt good. It felt good to hear those words come out of *his* mouth. I trusted him. He was one of the only men in my life, if not the only one, that I trusted wholeheartedly.

"You're ready for this," he said. "But there's a lot of responsibility that comes with it."

"I know, Coach," I said. "I'm ready."

"Good," he said with a proud smile much like how I imagined a father would smile at his son. "Get out there and get the guys warmed up. Tonight is another defense-heavy practice."

"Thanks, Coach," I said, "for believing in me."

"You got it, Son," he said in a fatherly tone.

Coach was the only person who called me "son" and I didn't mind it because he was real with me from the first day I met him. He was the only father figure I ever had. No, it wasn't like having a real dad that picked me up from school or watched the Knicks games with me, but it was better than nothing. And I appreciated having Coach in my life.

I left his office with a little more swagger than usual and went back into the locker room to tell the guys that it was time for practice. Leonard picked up on it. Tramon did too. I didn't even need to tell the guys that I had been named captain.

They followed Leonard, Tramon, and me out onto the floor. We took our positions at the heads of the stretching lines like before. Things were the same, but a little different at the same time. Me being the leader of the team was official now.

# FOUR

"You guys gotta sweat!" Coach yelled as he stalked up and down the floor during defensive stance drills.

"I don't care if it hurts!" he screamed. "Life hurts! Winning hurts! Passion hurts! You gotta want it!"

The guys behind me cussed at Coach under their breath. I turned back to glare at them. I wanted to make sure that everyone on *my* team was on the same page. We were going to work hard and we weren't going to complain about it. The guys behind me fixed their crooked faces and there wasn't any complaining after that. I looked over to Leonard and Tramon. Their eyes let me know they understood.

"Alright, relax," Coach finally said.

Everyone sighed in relief. The gym cooled down instantly as we stood up straight and relaxed our muscles. I gave each of my teammates a fist bump.

"Go get some water and then meet me at half court," Coach said to the team.

I didn't need water. I went straight to midcourt and Leonard came too.

"Practice is done," he said.

"What?" I asked and looked to the clock hanging on the wall. I hadn't realized that two hours had passed that quickly. We had spent the entire time working on defense. Coach didn't want practice to be longer than two hours, so a scrimmage seemed unlikely.

"I was focused," I said. "Shit. Time just flew."

"Yeah," Leonard said.

After the break, the rest of the team joined Leonard, Tramon, and me at midcourt. Coach had a strange, half-smiling, half-serious look on his face. I could usually read Coach pretty well, but I didn't recognize that expression. I didn't know what to expect.

"We're not gonna scrimmage tonight," he said. "You guys are done. I just wanted to say a few words to you guys before you go home."

Everyone's eyes were on him.

"I keep telling you guys that defense is hard and that life is hard. I want you to understand that. This isn't just about basketball. As much as you guys would like to believe otherwise, all of you aren't going to the NBA. I'm trying to teach you guys something about life so that you can live in the world. The real world."

He paused for a moment then paced while looking at the floor. He came back to his original spot and looked out at us again.

"Things are gonna happen in life that you don't expect. Things are gonna get in your way. But you can't complain and you can't just pack it in. You gotta keep moving. There's no time to feel sorry for yourself. Nobody wants to hear that. Nobody."

He paused one last time and crossed his arms over his chest.

"That's what this season is about. It's about what happens here," he said as he pointed to the floor. "But also, it's about what happens out there." He pointed to the doors that led outside the school.

"That's all, guys," he said. "Get home safe. And take care of your bodies. Be smart. See you tomorrow."

# FIVE

I took the train in the other direction to meet my mother at the diner on 130th. I was a little early, keeping up my trend of arriving on time, but didn't see her there. I waited for her outside the diner. It wasn't too cold—my body was still warm and almost numb because of the defensive drills—and I liked being outside, looking at the people as they walked by.

My mother was there right at seven thirty. I gave her a hug and kiss and we went inside and sat down in a booth by the front window.

The waitress brought out a couple of waters along with rolls and butter. The menus were already set on the table and my mother started looking through hers. I didn't need to look at mine.

"Meatloaf and mashed potatoes again?" she asked. "There are so many different things on this menu. Why don't you try something new?"

"No need. When something works, I stick to it," I said. "The meatloaf is on point."

She smiled and went back to her menu.

"I think I'm gonna get the lemon chicken," she said after a minute or two. "It's Greek."

I nodded and took a sip of my water.

She put down her menu and looked at me excitedly. Her eyes were lively and moving around quickly like she was anxious about something, but she also looked happy. I had forgotten how beautiful she was because she always looked so tired.

"How was your day?" she asked.

"It was good," I said. "School was . . . you know."

She rolled her eyes at that.

"But before practice, Coach called me into his office and we talked."

"About what?"

"He named me one of the captains for the season."

Her eyes lit up even more.

"Congratulations," she said.

"Thanks, Mom."

A moment passed where neither of us spoke. She took a sip of her water and cleared her throat.

"A lot of responsibility comes with something like this, Darnell," she said.

"I know, Mom."

She put a fist underneath her chin and stared at me for a second. She smiled. It always embarrassed me when she did that. I used to think that she did it to embarrass me.

"Would you stop?" I asked.

"You've come a long way," she said. "I'm proud of you. And I'm sure Coach is too."

"Thanks," I said before a big gulp of water. "How was *your* day?"

I smiled.

She rolled her eyes again and sighed.

"It was fine. Different day. Different case. Same stuff."

Our waiter came and took our order. I ordered lemonade and Mom ordered a glass of wine. The waiter brought the drinks out quickly.

"I wanted to talk to you about something," she said. "That's why I asked you to meet me here tonight."

"What's up?"

She took a deep breath and stared at me again before speaking.

"What is it?"

"I met someone, Darnell," she said.

After telling me that, she shut her eyes for a few beats like she was bracing for something. She opened her eyes and took a sip of her wine.

"That's why I've been coming home late some nights," she said.

I didn't say anything. I took a deep breath and looked past my mother. She didn't know that what she had done in the past caused me pain. There was no way for her to know. I never said anything.

I couldn't deal with my mother having a boyfriend. I would never meet him, even if she begged me to. And I *knew* I could never trust him. I wanted things to stay how they were—just my mother and me. That's how it was supposed to be and that's how it was going to stay.

"Darnell," she said. "Darnell?"

She took my hand. My eyes focused and met hers. I pulled my hand away. My eyes quickly shot down to the floor the way they did when I was a child and unable to defend myself.

"It's been a while, Darnell," she said. "When you were younger . . ."

She shook her head.

"After a while, I stopped dating because I was afraid of how you would react."

I stood up from the table and her eyes widened.

"I have to go," I said.

"Sit down," she said. "You're not going anywhere."

I turned around and walked out of the restaurant. I didn't look back as I walked down the stairs to the subway station. I got onto the first train headed back to Brooklyn. Once I sat down, I noticed that my mother had called and texted several times. I ignored the messages, put on some music, and slid my phone back into my pocket.

The music made me angrier for some reason. I turned it off, but left my headphones on. The rattling of the subway cars was the only sound underground. I didn't know where I was going. I didn't want to go home. I needed to walk around a little first.

I needed Brooklyn.

I got off the train at the first Brooklyn stop I

recognized, and when I got above ground, it was a little colder than before. The streets were alive, though, like always. It didn't matter that it was a weeknight. Brooklyn was always alive. I passed some crowded restaurants that looked new, and a few that looked like they had been there forever. There were people of every color hanging out, not just brown and black. Brooklyn was changing. I didn't know what that change meant, but it seemed to be changing for the better.

I passed by another restaurant with a big wooden bar at the front. I caught my reflection in the glass and realized that I looked like a grown man. Because I was meeting my mother for dinner, I changed back into my school uniform—khakis and a navy blue button down shirt—after practice. We couldn't wear hoodies or skullcaps at school, so I looked "proper" during the school week. I also had what my teammates liked to call a "grown man beard," not that patchy shit that you would see on most high school kids. Add to that the fact that people always assumed I was older because of my height and it was safe to say that I looked like a grown man. Check that. I was a grown man.

I saw the people at the bar laughing and having a good time. They were all white in a neighborhood that used to be all black. Staring at the bar made me thirsty. I went inside to get a drink. I was sure that if I carried myself the right way, the bartender would serve me.

I took a spot at the very end of the wooden bar. I took out a ten-dollar bill from my pocket. My mother had given it to me for snacks—healthy snacks—after school, but I still had the full ten dollars in tact. The bartender made his was over to me from the far end with a nod.

"What'll it be?" he asked with a wipe of the bar top.

"Yeah," I said. "Lemme have a beer."

"What kind?" he asked. "We have a huge selection of microbrews."

"I'll just take a Heineken."

He smirked and then his mouth tightened. "I'm sorry, we don't serve Heineken," he said. "I could show you a list of the beers we *do* have."

"Okay."

He handed me the list and I couldn't pronounce most of the names. They had beers from all over the world—France, Belgium, Germany. They even had a beer from South Africa. I just wanted a beer; I didn't want an adventure.

I called him back over and pointed at random to one of the beers on the list.

"Good choice," he said with a wink. "Would you like to see a food menu?"

"No, thanks," I said and he walked back down to middle of the bar.

I was hungry, but didn't have the cash. The thought of the meatloaf from the diner haunted me. I took out my phone and there were no new messages or calls from my mother.

The bartender brought the beer over and said that it was eight fifty. I almost sent it back. Eight dollars and fifty cents for a beer? For six fifty, I could've bought a six-pack of Heineken at the corner store near my apartment.

I gave him the ten and he left a dollar and two quarters on the bar. I took a sip of the beer and it was sour—the most sour thing I had ever tasted. But after the sourness went away, the aftertaste in my mouth was almost sweet and I felt refreshed. It took a little while to get used to, but I liked it. I looked around the restaurant and people were in their own little worlds. No one suspected that I was underage. No one seemed to give a damn that I bought a beer without being twenty-one.

This was my first beer in a while—since summer, actually. I decided at the end of the summer that I wasn't going to drink when the school year started and alcohol was certainly going to be off-limits during the season. But my mother's confession at the diner shook me all up. I needed something to calm me, and the sour beer from Belgium did that.

If certain people—Coach, my mother—found

out that I was having a beer in a bar, they'd be pissed, considering how important this year is for me. Coach would say, "Are you stupid or what?" My mother wouldn't say anything really; she'd just give me a smack in the mouth. But I didn't care. I needed that beer. And I wasn't worried. I would hold it together. I wouldn't let that one beer lead to something else. Something worse. I wasn't worried. Yet.

I finished the beer and a put the dollar and two quarters into my pocket. When I started walking toward the door, I had a little buzz on. The beer was stronger than I thought. It was a little colder outside when I hit the sidewalk. I rubbed my hands together and blew into them. I could feel the beer moving around in my empty stomach and the taste in my mouth was now stale and bitter. I spit onto the street a few times, but couldn't get the taste out. I needed food.

I walked around and found a 7-Eleven. I bought a hot dog and ate it in three bites. That helped my stomach a little but did nothing for the taste in my mouth. The flavor of the hot dog mixed with the bitterness made it even worse. The nice buzz I caught was turning into something mean and ugly; it rested down in the pit of my stomach, mixing with the beer and junk food. I started to sweat and looked up to the street sign above my head. Luckily, it rang a bell. I knew I was about forty minutes away from my apartment on foot. I didn't have any more money for the subway. I wiped the sweat from my forehead and started on my way home.

About twenty minutes into my walk, my mother texted me again, asking where I was. I texted back, and told her that I was in Brooklyn walking to the apartment. She replied that she was home waiting up for me and that we weren't finished talking.

I had to make sure that my breath didn't smell like beer when I got home. I slid into a corner store and bought a pack of cinnamon gum. I chewed the whole pack until I got to the apartment.

When I got to the door, I didn't even need to knock for her to open up. She was already in front of it, listening for my steps. Her eyes were serious when I walked inside—half-angry, half-concerned.

"Boy, don't you ever get up and walk out on me like that again," she said.

I didn't reply.

"Where did you go?"

"I went for a walk."

"Did you eat?"

I shook my head.

"I brought your meatloaf home," she said. "It's in the fridge. I'll heat it—"

"It's okay," I said. "I'm fine."

She took a deep breath and walked over to me.

"Let's sit," she said.

We both sat down on the couch. She took another deep breath and pinned her hair behind her ears. She always did that when she had something that she wanted to say. When I was a kid and she'd want to tell me something that was hard—like when my dad took off—she would pin her hair behind her ears.

"You're not a little kid anymore, Darnell," she said. "You're a grown man. You're getting ready to go to college."

I still didn't say anything.

"I haven't had a boyfriend in six years," she said. "And it's hard being alone."

Her eyes started to tear up around the edges.

"And now that you're leaving soon," she said, "I can't be alone. It ain't fair to ask me to be."

I couldn't stand to see her cry. I tried to stand up from the couch but she stopped me. I looked away from her.

"Do you understand, Darnell?" she asked. "You're not a little kid anymore. You have to grow up."

I opened my mouth to speak. I was ready to speak, but something stopped me. My mind was ready to talk, but something held me back. I didn't want to hurt her with the past. She had been through enough already.

"What?" she asked. "What do you want to say?"

I sighed heavily, but said nothing.

The water around her eyes formed into a few tears. She wiped them away before leaning over and kissing me on the cheek. I could feel the hot wetness of her face as it was close to mine. She pulled away and went into her room. Soon after, her light was off and she was in bed. I stayed out in the living room for probably another fifteen minutes, just sitting quietly. I knew that my mother couldn't be alone forever. I didn't want that for her. I wanted her to be happy. But there was something else inside of me fighting against that. I felt threatened by my mother's new boyfriend and I didn't even know him. I stared at the blank TV screen not knowing what to do.

# SIX

I woke up late the next morning and my mother did too. She got ready in a rush and left without having breakfast. The only thing she said before heading out the door was, "Text me after practice to let me know about tonight." It *was* Friday and usually that was the night the two of us went to the movies. It was kind of like our little family tradition. Since she had a boyfriend, though, I had to text her after practice and let her know about it.

I finished my cereal and looked at the clock. So much for my early streak. I knew I was gonna hear something about this from Coach. I got myself together and left the apartment. The subway station was packed because of some delays, and this would probably add to my tardiness. There was nothing else to do but put my headphones in and wait. No use in worrying.

When the train finally showed, it was a mad rush to get on and there were no open seats. It was cramped inside the car as usual, and on top of that, someone opened some nasty-smelling food and it stunk up the whole car. I couldn't wait to get off of that train, holding my nose and closing my eyes tight. There was another delay in the middle of a tunnel and we were stuck in the dark for a little while. The conductor tried to give an explanation, but the speakers were shot. Everyone on the train rolled their eyes at the half-hearted, static-filled explanation.

The car started up again and the conductor offered his apologies, but apologies wouldn't save my ass from being late to school. With my stop coming up, I forced my way to a spot right next to the door as if saving seconds would be the difference between being on time or late for first bell. I was the first one off when the train stopped and I took the stairs two at a time until reaching street level. I checked my phone and I still had five minutes before first bell. If I ran, there was a chance I could make it. So I ran. I nearly slammed into some folks on the sidewalk as I reached a full sprint.

The front door of school was in sight with three minutes to spare. There was no way I was going to be late now. I was on the opposite side of the street just one block away from school, and there was a choice to be made: either wait for the light to cross the intersection legally or say *fuck it*, cross the middle of the street, and walk right into the front door of school on time.

I took a quick peek over at the light at the intersection. It was known to take forever to change.

I said *fuck it*.

I stepped off the curb and onto the street with one minute before first bell. There were cars coming on both sides and they were going fast—not fifty miles per hour or anything like that—but fast enough to badly hurt a nigga who was trying like hell to get to school on time.

I saw my opening. I crossed the street and made it to the middle. There was just enough room there to wait for the other side to clear.

I could hear the cars rushing by behind me, the drivers honking angrily and shouting cuss words in my direction out their windows. There was no opening to get across the other side, so I waited uncomfortably.

Finally, a car down at the intersection hesitated and I had my chance. I misjudged how far away it was, though. The car picked up speed and headed straight for me. I heard the blast of its horn and I dove out of the street onto the sidewalk in front of school. I heard tires swerving and then the collision. I looked back into the street and there was chaos.

"What were you thinking?" Coach said in his office.

"I just . . . " I said. "I just wanted to be on time."

He looked at me like I was crazy, like the idea of risking my life in order to catch first bell was the stupidest decision a person could make.

"That car came this close to taking you apart," he said, holding his pointer and middle fingers about an inch apart. "The driver is gonna be okay, but his car and the car that he slammed into, they're totaled."

"I'm sorry, Coach," I said.

"I'm not gonna lecture you right now," he said. "Quite frankly, you're too old to be lectured anymore."

I was tired of people telling me to grow up. But I knew I was going to continue hearing it until I did.

"But this is what I meant, when we talked before the first practice," he said. "You can't be taken serious when you do shit like this. Not in the locker room. Not in the world."

"I know, Coach," I said. "I'll grow up."

"I can't trust you, Darnell," he said. "You can't be a captain pulling shit like this. I told you to be on time. I told you to be responsible."

"But Coach—"

He put his hand up to silence me.

"I . . . the school, we have to try to clean this up," he said. "After we're done here, go home. I have to talk to the principal and see what we're going to do about this. You're excused from today and tomorrow's practice. Sunday we're off. I'll let you know on Monday if you're still on the team and allowed back at school."

"Coach," I said weakly.

"You gotta be accountable, Darnell."

"Coach."

He pointed toward to the door.

"Go home," he said without looking at me. "I'll call you."

I turned to leave.

"Darnell," Coach said. "I'll call your mother and tell her the news. Because I know you won't."

I left the office and then school. I got on the train and headed back to the neighborhood.

# SEVEN

Coach was right, I wouldn't tell my mother what happened if I didn't have to, but there was no getting out this. Coach would tell her and I would be getting a call or text any minute.

I didn't hear from her while I was on the train, but I knew there wasn't much time. I stopped by the house to change clothes. On the way out of my room, the view outside the window caught my eye. You could see Manhattan clear across the river that day. The sky was perfect.

I charged my phone for five minutes and left the house. It was about noon. My friends from school were obviously not around to hang out with. I decided to check up on one of my best friends from around the neighborhood instead.

Even though my mother and I lived in the same apartment for my whole life, I stopped going to school in the neighborhood at age twelve. Basketball was my ticket to private schools. And it was a good thing, too. The neighborhood was really different in those days. Everything was crumbling: the buildings, the sidewalks, even the people. But the neighborhood changed with time. There were stores, restaurants, and new houses. People looked good. They were out in the streets with smiles on their faces. Things seemed more connected.

I didn't see my old friends from around the neighborhood all that much during the school year because of basketball. I would spend most of the summer with them though. We'd party, chase girls, and generally be up to no good. Nothing crazy, just young fun.

I texted my best friend, Manny, and he replied

that he wasn't home. He was my age but not in school. He dropped out right before junior year. He wasn't a bum or anything like that; he just wanted to work instead of going to school. His dream was to open a restaurant one day in the neighborhood and he was building that dream with a waiter job at a restaurant a few blocks away.

*Stop by the restaurant if u can*, Manny wrote.

*Ok.*

*And can u grab a blunt? I have a break coming up.*

*Yeah.*

He gave me walking directions to his restaurant.

I still had no calls or texts from my mother.

I hit the first corner store in sight and grabbed the blunt. I found the restaurant right where Manny said it was. I looked in the window and saw him in his black T-shirt and black slacks. I wasn't used to seeing him all official like that. I walked in and caught his attention with a nod.

I hadn't seen him since the summer when his hair was down to his shoulders and his beard flowed in black curls all around his face. His hair was cut close now and the beard was all gone. Manny was my only Puerto Rican friend from the neighborhood. He lived with his grandmother, who raised him because his mother died from an overdose. Like me, he never met his father.

"What up, D?" he said, approaching with a wide grin on his face.

"Just hangin' out in the BK," I said.

I wasn't down because of the trouble at school or even because my mother was going to kill me when she found out. The sun was out. It was Friday. I was free.

"Why aren't you at school?" he asked.

"I'll tell you when you get that break."

"That's a bet," he said. "Gimme ten."

I nodded and walked out to the side of the restaurant. I waited near the mouth of an alley where a pack of skateboarders, most likely cutting school, smoked cigarettes and talked shit with one another.

Manny appeared right next to me with that wide grin on his face.

"Follow me," he said.

We walked down the alley, then took a sharp right before the end of it. Manny had found a safe place to get high while he was at work. The spot was in between two walls that surrounded a couple of small parking lots on both sides. We were hidden in every direction.

"You got it?" he asked.

I put the blunt in his hand. I told him the story of what happened at school as he cracked it open and rolled it back up with marijuana inside. He looked up every now then when the story got good, his eyes wide and mouth curled into that unforgettable Caribbean smile.

"So you kicked out of school for this stunt?" he asked before sealing the blunt with his spit.

"I don't know," I said.

"They ain't gonna kick you out, son," he said. "You're too important to the team. And that's what really matters."

He fired up his lighter and put it across the blunt. Then he put the blunt to his lips and set fire to it.

"My mom is gonna go crazy when she finds out," I said. "That's why I left the pad so fast. I'm thinking of not going home to face the music until Sunday."

"That's smart," he said as he took a big hit and let the smoke settle in his chest.

"I got somewhere to stay tomorrow night," I said. "This chick from school. But tonight, I don't know."

He held the blunt out to me and I took it.

"You're just gonna have to see where tonight takes you then," he said before coughing violently.

I took a small hit. My lungs wouldn't have been able to take one bigger than that. My body was used to being in prime shape during the school year. I let the smoke creep out of my lungs through my mouth and nose.

"I'll party for two days and then go home Sunday to deal with it," I said. "Whatever it is."

I handed the blunt back to Manny and he shook his head in agreement.

———

Manny went back to work and we planned on meeting up after he got off at five o'clock. It was already one in the afternoon and the fact that I didn't have any calls or texts from my mother yet made me wonder. Coach obviously hadn't told her the news yet and she would be expecting a text from me at some point that day to let her know about movie night. I wasn't sure what to do.

If *I* picked up my phone and told her about being sent home from school, it would trigger a never-ending flow of calls and texts from her.

If I didn't say anything about the accident and she found out from Coach, I'd be in even more trouble for lying.

I decided to wait it out.

The other thing I had to do was figure out how to kill four hours. Even though I didn't have that much of it, the weed had me feeling funny. I needed to do something to get the fog out of my head. I needed to sweat. There were a couple of parks around that part of Brooklyn, so I went looking for them.

I found one of the parks and the basketball courts not too far inside. I hadn't played on those courts since I was ten, but as soon as I saw them, the memories came back. On one side, there were four guys playing two-on-two. They looked a little bit older than me, but not by much. I looked around to see if there were three other guys to jump in to make a five-on-five full court game, but there wasn't anyone around.

I walked over to them and waited for a break

in the action to call "next." The guy who had the ball looked familiar, but I couldn't put a name to the face. I watched him school the rest of the guys. His handle was smooth and his shot was nice too. He was by far the best player on the court.

He finished the game with a step-back jumper and after slapping five with the other three players on the court, he walked over to me.

"Darnell?" he asked.

"Yeah," I said.

I narrowed my eyes to get a closer look at him.

"Do we know each other?" I asked.

He smiled and held his hand up next to his hip. "Man, I used to coach you when you were this big!"

We shook hands and I looked at him some more. Still couldn't place him.

"I don't remember," I said.

"It was a long time ago," he said. "You were

probably, nine, ten years old. The old rec-league in Park Slope they used to have for kids?"

"Oh, that's right," I said, flashing back on those years.

He looked young to be a coach.

"What's your name again?"

"Ron," he said. "Y'all used to call me 'Coach Ron.'"

"Now, I remember," I said. "We used to play at that old rec center, MLK park."

"Yeah," he said. "Tuesday and Thursday nights."

"They still have that league?"

"Nah," he said. "They don't. But hey, how is your mother doing? I remember she used to be real protective of you. And she wanted us to be hard on you. Toughen you up."

"She good," I said with a chuckle. "That definitely sounds like her."

"Well, it's taken you far," he said. "You're a hell of a player. I've been watching."

"Thanks."

A confused look came across his face. "Why aren't you in school right now?"

I clapped my hands theatrically. "Oh, there were teacher meetings today. We had the day off."

He nodded.

"But I got practice tonight," I added. "Just wanted to come around the way and get an extra run in."

He smiled and pointed at the guys that he just finished playing with. "Pick one of those chumps that just lost and let's go."

"They can just shoot for it," I said.

One of the players from the losing team snatched the ball from Ron and the two of them starting shooting for the other spot on my team.

I tied my shoes up tight, pulled my belt even tighter around my jeans, and loosened my muscles a little. Ron walked over to me and patted me on the back.

"Don't go too hard now," he said. "I don't

want you getting hurt out here before your practice tonight. This season is big for you."

I couldn't tell him the truth. I couldn't tell him that I had been sent home from school for a silly incident. I couldn't tell him that I just got finished smoking a blunt.

"Yeah," I said to him, cussing myself out in my own head. "It is big."

———

The teams split the first two games, with Ron's team winning the first one and my team taking the second. Ron and I pretty much scored all of the points for our teams, but that didn't stop the two other guys from playing hard.

"One more?" Ron asked after the second game.

There was no way around playing a third game. You don't leave the court with a tie. It just doesn't work that way. It doesn't matter if you're uptown at a Y or at the park in BK.

I nodded my head. "Don't even need to ask."

The third game started with me scoring the first six points and shutting Ron down when they were on offense. The games were first team to sixteen by ones and you had to win by two.

By the time Ron shook free from my defense and sank a jumper for their first basket, it was ten to one. I blocked his layup attempt on the next possession and scored three more baskets for us. On the next possession, I got past Ron with a crossover, left to right, and found my teammate under the basket for a slam. It was fourteen to one and then fourteen to five when I stole the ball from Ron and hit a deep jumper to put us up fifteen to five.

There was no trash talking out there. Growing up and playing outside always brought out a little trash talking, but this was a little different. Ron had reminded me that he was a coach of mine and it triggered the respect for coaches that I had inside of me. I was never one to disrespect coaches growing up. My coaches throughout the years were my father figures, so once Ron told me that he was an old coach of mine, there was no way I was going to talk shit to him. Besides, he was a good player—good enough to hold his own against me.

We checked the ball and it was time for me to end the game. I dribbled to the left of the key and called for my teammate to come out high and set a screen for me. Ron anticipated the screen to come on the right and at the last second I went away from it with a crossover from right to left.

I had a step on Ron and a clear lane along the left baseline. When I elevated toward the rim, the other defender came over to try and block the shot. I flew by him and scored the final bucket of the game with a reverse layup on the other side of the rim.

We won sixteen to five. That was the series.

The four of us shook hands and had a few laughs. As we walked off the court and left the park, Ron lagged behind the other two and walked with me.

"You got that strong game," he said. "You play like a man."

"You got game too," I said.

"Shit," he said. "I'm an old man compared to you."

"How often do you guys run out here?"

"We come out as much as we can," he said. "We all work, so you know."

"Yeah," I said.

"You gotta get over to school for practice," he said with a chuckle. "At least you're already warmed up."

"Yeah, that's true," I said, looking down to the ground.

"It was good seeing you, Darnell," he said. We shook hands and half-hugged. "Keep doing your thing. I'm gonna follow your career. I know you'll do Brooklyn proud. A lot of these young niggas, they countin' on you."

I nodded, but deep down, with all the shit swirling around and inside of me, I didn't believe what he said. I wasn't making Brooklyn proud. I wasn't making the people who cared about me proud.

Ron and I stood at the entrance of the park. The sidewalks and streets were crowded now. There were kids fresh out of school looking forward to the weekend, and there were adults of all colors getting an early jump on things in the cafes and restaurants.

"Neighborhood's changed," he said.

I nodded.

"Take care of yourself," he said.

We shook again and he started to walk away to join his two friends up ahead.

"Ron!" I said.

He turned and looked back at me.

"How did you coach so young?" I asked. "I mean, you must've only been in high school when you coached me, and you *still* look young now."

"I *was* young," he said with a smile. "I was seventeen years old when I was your coach"

"Damn! How'd they let you coach at that age?"

He smiled again.

"I had to," he said.

"You had to?"

"The state of New York said I had to. I got into some trouble around the way, got myself kicked out of school, and it was either coach kids in basketball while I got my GED, or Boys Village."

I didn't say anything.

"Easy choice," he said before turning around and walking off.

I checked my phone and it was four thirty. There were ten texts and five calls from my mother. They weren't about movie night. Coach had told her about me getting sent home from school. She was pissed.

The phone buzzed in my hand and it was her again. I refused the call and put it on silent.

I couldn't deal with everything all at once. I needed to take my mind off of it.

I went back to the restaurant to meet up with Manny.

# EIGHT

"What's the plan?" I asked Manny as he changed his shirt in the alley next to the restaurant. He took his black shirt and put it in his book bag. Now that it was dark out, he rolled another blunt out in the open and we smoked it freely. I took more smoke into my lungs this time and was punished for it with violent, dry coughs.

"I hit up this girl from up by Fort Green," he said before taking a long pull from the blunt. "I told her to grab a friend."

He coughed as he offered the blunt back to me. I waved it off.

"And?"

"She's working on it," he said.

"So what are we gonna do in the mean time?"

"Well, I told her that if she gets a friend, that we would bring the shit that gets you fucked up."

"That was your deal with her?"

"That was my deal," he said in that confident way that only a Puerto Rican from Brooklyn could have.

"Let's roll then," I said.

"Let's do it," he said.

We walked down the busy sidewalk on the street that Manny's restaurant was on and things were just getting started in there. The bar was packed with white men in suits and women in dresses. The tables were the same story. I tapped Manny on his back as we walked by.

"You should be working at night, son," I said. "That's when you can make the real money."

"If I was working now," he said with hazy eyes, "I wouldn't be able to get fucked up with you."

When we got back to the neighborhood, it was

completely dark and the temperature had dropped. We passed my building and I looked up to see no lights on in my apartment.

I took my phone out of my pocket and stared at it.

"What are you doing just standing there?" Manny asked.

"Oh. Nothing. I'm gonna go upstairs and grab a jacket," I said. "You wanna come up or wait?"

"Nah," he said. "I'm gonna go see what's up with Mike. If we're gonna go meet these chicas later, we need some more bud."

"Mike still sells bud?"

"That's all he does," he said. "He barely leaves the house anymore. He's paranoid."

I shook my head.

"Paranoid?" I asked. "Over selling bud?"

"He sells the white too," he said.

I nodded.

"I'll catch you over there," I said.

He nodded back and continued down the

sidewalk. I ran up the stairs to my building and went through the front door.

My mother and I used to meet at the apartment on Friday evenings. We were always exhausted from our weeks at work and school, but we'd always find the energy to go out for dinner and a movie. The apartment was dark and empty when I opened the door. Things were changing.

I quickly went to work, changing my shirt and grabbing a jacket. A sudden wave of hunger came over me. I made my way into the kitchen and looked in the fridge. There wasn't much in there. That was odd. My mother always kept the fridge full. But she had a boyfriend now.

I threw a sandwich together with what was in there and ate it in one minute. I realized that the sandwich was the first thing I had eaten since breakfast. If I was in school that day, that never would've happened. I needed food—a lot of food—to get through a full day of classes and then basketball.

I cleaned up the kitchen and left the apartment.

By the time my foot hit the pavement in front of my building, it was six thirty. I checked my phone and there were five more texts and two more calls from my mother. She demanded that I call her. There were also three texts from Jessica. In the first one, she asked why I wasn't in school and that there was a crazy rumor floating around that I was kicked out of school for doing drugs. In the second one, she asked me if the rumor was true. And finally in the third one, she asked me if I was going to come over on Saturday.

I didn't reply to any of the stuff about me being sent home from school. I only answered her last question about Saturday.

*I'll be there tomorrow.*

I tried to justify ignoring my mother's texts and missed calls. *If she wanted to know what was going on with me, she would have been home and not at her boyfriend's house.*

I put my phone, still on silent, back in my pocket.

Mike's place was a few blocks up on the left. His apartment was right next door to the one that he grew up in with his mother. The only difference between the buildings was that Mike's was newer. Around the time when he really started dealing a lot of weed, it seemed like new apartment buildings were going up in Brooklyn by the week. When Mike started making a little cash for himself, he decided that he wanted to move out of his mama's house. And in true Brooklyn fashion, he moved right next door to his mother. If he ever missed her or her cooking, he could get his lazy ass up off the couch and walk next door to see her.

That was Brooklyn in a nutshell. At least to me it was.

I knocked on the door to Mike's apartment, flashing back on the last time I was there. It was two summers before and he was having a party with people from the neighborhood. It was just a small party, but there was a lot of weed and liquor. From the few details I could remember, it was a good night.

Mike answered the door and a smile cut across his naturally frowning face. "What up, D? Long time."

We shook hands and I followed him inside. Manny was sitting on the couch with a pipe in his hand. Even though the apartment was dark, I could see the redness around Manny's eyes. I took a seat on the chair next to the couch and Mike sat down next to Manny. Everything in his apartment—the TV, the entertainment center, the couches—looked new.

"Where you been?" Mike asked with another rare smile. "You big-timin' it now? Forgettin' where you came from and shit?"

There was no anger or jealousy in his voice.

"Nah, it ain't like that," I said with a smile of my own.

"Manny told me you got some shit goin' on at school right now," he said. "Tryin' to take your mind off things."

I didn't say anything.

"I got you," he said.

He pulled a little bag of weed out of a small drawer on his coffee table. He handed me the bag.

"Smell that shit," Manny said, still holding the pipe even though there was no weed left in the bowl. "The shit is dank."

I smelled it and he was right. It was some of the funkiest weed I'd ever smelled.

I handed the little bag back to Mike.

"You get all this shit from selling weed?" I asked with a nod to the entertainment center.

"Mostly," he said. "Other shit too."

I looked over to Manny and he looked away.

"Other shit?" I asked. "Like what?"

"Don't worry about it," Mike said.

"Be careful with the hard shit, Mike," I said. "They'll lock your black ass up and won't think twice."

"They ain't lockin' me up," he said. "I keep my shit tight."

I looked back at Manny. "What's up with the chicas from Fort Green?"

"Ah," he said. "She just texted back and said she's got a nice friend for you. Big titties. Fat ass. Just the way you *negros* like it."

"We'll see," I said, turning back to Mike. "Last time this so-called Puerto Rican pimp tried to hook me up, she had a mustache. I didn't stick around to find out, but I bet she had a big dick, too."

Mike cracked up at that. Manny did too with the empty pipe still in his hand. The weed was starting to hit him. Mike's shit was strong.

Manny sat up and placed the pipe down on the table. He rubbed his face, eyes, and mouth.

"This *boricua* is fucked up," I said. "Holding onto a pipe with no weed in it for like fifteen minutes."

Mike laughed again.

"We gotta go," Manny said as he stood up from the couch. "We gotta go get liquor for the girls."

I stood up and so did Mike. We all shook hands.

"We need to kick it more, D," Mike said.

"If things don't go my way at school," I said, "you'll definitely be seeing more of me around the neighborhood."

When we reached the door, I turned back to Mike.

"Watch out, Mike. Don't get too deep in this shit."

"Gotchu, all-star," he said with one final smile.

"And get some light in here," I said. "I can barely see your black ass."

He pushed me out of the door and closed it shut. It was seven o'clock when we hit the street. We had to find a liquor store that would sell to us. There would be no girls without liquor, and there would be no party without girls.

———

The first two liquor stores we tried wouldn't give in. Both times I went in by myself because Manny looked too young. Both clerks didn't believe that I had forgotten my ID and sent me away empty-handed. We decided that it would be best to get up to Fort Green and try the liquor stores there. Maybe there we could get someone who didn't know our faces to buy the liquor for us.

When we got to Fort Green, two more liquor store clerks shut us down. After the second denial, Manny, nervous because he knew he needed the liquor to be successful with his girl, kicked a brick wall.

"We gotta just take the shit and run, man," he said.

"What?"

"Yeah."

"What are we gonna do? Walk behind the counter and say, 'Excuse me, sir, I'm just gonna take your shit,' and walk out of there?"

"No," he said. "We have to find one where the liquor isn't behind the register."

I gave him a crooked look.

"Come on," he said.

We walked a couple more blocks and found another store on the corner.

"I'll go in first," he said. "If I'm in there more than a few minutes, that means it's a go."

"It's a go?" I asked. "What do you mean?"

"I'll grab the shit," he said, and his eyes were suddenly focused. "And after a few minutes, come in and buy a pack of gum." He shook his head. "Better yet, buy blunts. We need those too."

"You sure about this?"

"Yeah, D," he said. "You said you wanted to get crazy, right?"

"Yeah, alright," I said. "Just don't get my ass locked up for some stupid shit like this. I don't even need the alcohol to get pussy."

"Whatever, man," he said. "You in or out?"

"Go on in there!" I said with a shove to his back.

He went inside and I watched him through the glass door as he started looking around at the racks of liquor in the back of the store. He walked out of sight and stayed there for a couple of minutes. That was my signal to go in.

When I did, I glanced to the back of the store and saw him there in front of one of the shelves stocked with liquor. I turned to the cash register at the front and there was one guy buying a pack of cigarettes. I waited behind him, trying not to look back at Manny. He took his cigarettes from the clerk and walked out of the store.

It was my turn at the register. I asked for three blunts. When the clerk turned around to grab them from the cigar rack, I turned back and Manny was starting to make his way to the front of the store. I turned back around at the same time the clerk did and noticed that the Black & Mild's on the cigar rack were lower than the blunts. The clerk would have to bend down to pick those, giving Manny enough time to get out of the store safely.

"And, uh, lemme get a few Black and Mild's," I said.

"You got it," the clerk said.

He turned back to the rack and bent down. I blindly waved Manny to get out of the store.

And Manny, to his credit, didn't run out of the store like a guilty thief. He just walked at a quick pace, and by the time the clerk stood up and turned back to face me, Manny was out of the store.

"Four fifty," the clerk said.

"Keep it," I said, handing him a five-dollar bill.

I walked out of the store and looked around for him. He wasn't in front of the store—another smart move. I continued down the block until I saw an alley. That's where I found him with his jacket bulging with bottles.

# NINE

We got to the girl's house. It was one of those old, two-story brownstones that you see all over the BK. She answered the door after a few knocks. She smiled when she saw Manny and revealed a chipped front tooth. I thought it was cute and Manny seemed to as well.

We walked inside and the house was dark except for the flashing light that came from the television in the living room. Inside the living room was my girl. She was sitting on the couch.

I couldn't tell much other than that she had dark black hair.

"Can we turn some lights on?" I said to no one in particular.

I wanted to see exactly what I was dealing with.

"Sure," Manny's girl said.

She flicked a switch and the overhead lights kicked on.

My girl got up off the couch and walked over to me.

"This is Gabriela," Manny's girl said.

"Hello," I said.

"Hi," Gabriela said.

Her hair was long and it flowed down to the middle of her back.

And as she got close to me, I could smell her perfume or whatever it was that she had sprayed all over herself. It was sweet—probably too sweet—but I didn't complain.

Her breasts were big, just like Manny said. I could see the roundness of them underneath her tight, black, long-sleeve shirt. They weren't too big though. They were the perfect size.

"Turn around," I said.

She turned around to show me her ass. It was perfect too. Not too big, nothing outrageous.

"Let's have a drink," Manny said from behind us. "And then let's roll a little something."

His girl laughed and they left the living room and walked into the kitchen. Gabriela turned back around to face me.

"What did Manny's girl tell you about me?" I asked.

"Nothing," she said.

"Come on."

She bit her bottom lip and I remember thinking it was sexy.

"She said you're a big basketball star," she said.

"At least you're honest."

"I don't care about any of that," she said. "I just want to party."

"Okay," I said.

We walked into the kitchen together and Manny and his girl were busy making drinks.

Manny had stole a bottle of rum along with a bottle of vodka from the corner store and his girl was busy cutting and smashing these little green leaves. After she finished doing that, she threw a little bit of the leaves into the bottom of four drinking glasses. Then she put a little bit of sugar into each of the glasses. Manny was busy squeezing the juice from limes into a measuring cup.

"This is a Caribbean classic, right here, D," Manny said. "But I learned a little trick from the bartender at my restaurant."

Manny's girl put what looked like a little wooden baseball bat into each of the four glasses. She smashed the leaves and sugar together and then Manny poured some lime juice into each of the glasses. Next, he poured rum—a lot of rum—into each glass.

"Here's the trick, *mira, chicas,*" he said. "A splash of club soda at the end."

Manny handed each one of us a glass. He raised his in the air and the rest of us followed.

"*Saludos*," he said to the girls. Then looking at me, "And to our darker-colored friends, cheers!"

We knocked glasses and drank. The drink tasted amazing. There was a sharp bite of liquor, but the other flavors were strong too.

"This shit is good, son!" I said.

"I'm glad you like it," he said with that wide smile. "Ladies, you don't know what we had to do to get these drinks in your hands."

His girl leaned into him and Gabriela did the same to me.

"Let's roll one," he said.

I handed him the blunts and he went to work. He was a natural. He worked like a surgeon when it came to rolling. Manny was put on this earth to roll blunts the way I was made to play basketball.

He split the first cigar open and emptied the tobacco out onto a plate. He took the little bag of weed that we got from Mike and pulled out a few buds. The skunky smell of the weed quickly filled the room. It was so strong that Gabriela's nose twitched when the smell hit it. Manny pulled all of the leaves off of the buds and piled them into the wrapper. He shifted the wrapper in circles, careful not to spill any weed or crack the wrapper.

He sealed the blunt and then repeated the process for blunt number two. The three of us just sat there watching him as he worked. When he was almost done with the second one, I finished my drink with a large gulp. The alcohol went straight to my head and the buzz I was looking for had arrived. I looked over to Gabriela. She caught my glance and smiled at me. I put my hand on her ass and left it there. The "evil"—a saying my summer friends and I liked to use—was starting to get me, and there was no way I could stop it.

"Okay," Manny said after sealing the second blunt. "One for you two, and one for us. This will be enough for the four of us tonight. I just had one little hit at Mike's and it fuuuuuuuucked me up!"

The girls giggled and Manny handed me one of the blunts.

"Now, D, if you'll excuse me," he said before a large sip of his drink, "me and this little girl have some business to handle."

He took her by the waist and they started to leave the kitchen.

"Help yourself to more liquor," he said. "You probably won't need it; the weed is righteous."

Manny and his girl walked upstairs, leaving Gabriela and I standing there alone in the kitchen.

———

"Where's a lighter?" I asked her.

She took one from her purse on the little table in front of the couch in the living room.

"What's your friend's name?" I asked. "Manny's girl. I didn't catch it."

She smiled. "Maria."

"Where are her folks?"

"They're on vacation," she said. "In Puerto Rico."

"Cool. Cool."

I lit the blunt and took a pull. It rattled my chest and I started coughing as I passed it over to Gabriela. She took it from me and took two little puffs, and then a third, bigger one. She took the smoke into her lungs and held it there. She didn't cough. She was a pro.

"This is good shit," she said, blowing smoke out through her mouth and nose.

She passed it back to me.

I took a couple more pulls and they made me cough even more. My body wasn't used to the "evil" during the season and was fighting against it.

"So are you a star?" she asked after I passed the blunt back to her.

"I was," I said. "And I guess we'll have to wait and see if I'll stay one."

"What does that mean?" she asked before a few more puffs.

"Some shit went down at school," I said. "Some stupid shit."

I brought the bottle of rum into the living room and refilled my glass. I didn't have the patience to make the fancy drink that Manny and Maria made before. Gabriela's glass didn't need a refill yet.

"That shit'll pass," she said.

"That's why I'm here right now," I said before taking a sip of my rum. It stung going down. The "evil" was getting stronger and stronger by the second.

"Come here," she said. "Come close to me."

I leaned in close to her. She put the lit part of the blunt into her mouth and bit down on the wet end. She pulled my arm to come even closer and I did. We were face to face. I leaned in for the shotgun and she blew a thick stream of smoke straight down into my lungs. And that was that. The "evil" owned my body and mind.

She took the blunt out of her mouth and put it out. She finished her drink in one thunderous try.

"And now," she said, "I'm fucked up."

She stood up from the couch, took a few wobbly steps away from it, and took off her shirt. She was wearing nothing else but a bra and the tops of her breasts were popping out of it. Her skin was white, but not too white, it had just the right amount of color in it.

"You wanna see them?" she asked.

I nodded slowly and she tossed her shirt at me.

She unfastened her bra and her breasts came spilling out. My first glance was right. They were perfect in shape and size, just big enough to fill the palm of your hand. She walked back over to the couch and sat down in my lap. She kissed me hard on the mouth, pushing her tongue into mine. It was a sloppy kiss, but I didn't give a damn.

———

"Yo, D," a whispering voice said. "D."

I opened my eyes slowly and saw Manny outlined at the entrance of the living room. It was still dark out for the most part, and the room was too. I was lying on the couch with Gabriela on top of me, naked. Through a bluish tint in the room, I could see her perfectly round ass at the end of the couch. Underneath her, I was naked too.

Manny walked carefully into the room to see if I was awake. I flashed my eyes at him and he leaned in close to my right ear.

"Come into the kitchen," he whispered. "Let's roll another one."

"I'll meet you in there," I said. "I need to find my clothes."

He smiled and walked out of the living room.

I moved slowly, trying not to wake Gabriela up. I slid out from under her and she dropped softly onto the couch. She didn't wake up, just snored a little as she repositioned herself.

I found my clothes and put them on. I took my cell phone from the table in front of the couch. I checked the time and it was four a.m. There was only one new text from my mother—a long one. She explained that she too didn't go home that night and that the only thing she wanted at that point was to know I was safe.

*I'm safe, Mom*, I wrote back to her.

Jessica had texted me twice. The first one said that she was gonna "rock my world" and the second asked me if I was even going to show up. I put my phone back down on the table and walked into the kitchen.

Manny was finished rolling the blunt when I got in there and he sparked it.

"What'd you get Black and Mild's for?" he asked in a low and scratchy voice. "I hate 'em."

"I got them so your Puerto Rican ass could get out of that liquor store without getting caught."

We both chuckled as he handed the blunt over to me.

"This shit is strong," he said.

I nodded as I took a hit.

"Did you crush?" he asked.

I blew the smoke out through my mouth. No cough this time.

"Whatchu think?" I asked before taking another pull. "She's butt-ass naked in there, lying on top of me."

"She's so hot, man."

I passed the blunt back to him and he took a few little hits.

"That's funny how you can sleep with a super fine girl and just pass it off like it's nothing."

"What am I supposed to do?" I asked. "I know she's fine, but it's no big thing."

He shook his head.

"I don't make girls my everything," I said. "I mean, don't get me wrong, I love the company of a female. But I think there is more to life than that."

"Like what?" he asked. "Basketball?"

"Yeah," I said. "But even that is up in the air for me right now. Fuck, man."

He tried to hand the blunt back to me but I waved it off. I had to clear my throat and put my forearm to my mouth to muffle the sound.

Manny took one more hit and then put it out in the sink. He took the butt and dropped it into the empty rum bottle. He gathered up all of the mess we had made the night before and placed it on one part of the counter.

"I'll clean this shit when it's light out," he said.

He put the plate that the he had rolled the blunts on into the sink and ran some water over it. He took a rag from the sink and wiped down the counter.

"Yo, D," he said after dropping the rag back into the sink. "What are you gonna do if basketball doesn't work out for you?"

"I don't know, man," I said. "I don't really wanna even think about it."

He didn't say anything to that.

"I guess I'll find out on Sunday," I said.

He gave me a pat on the shoulder.

"What about you?" I asked.

"Me?" he asked. "I'm gonna work at this restaurant for as long as I can and you know, move up. Brooklyn is changing. People wanna be out and they wanna eat at these fancy places."

"Yeah," I said. "I see that."

"And then, you know, I'm gonna open my own place one day. One right in the neighborhood. And then one in Manhattan. Could you imagine that—a kid like me with his own place in Manhattan?"

"That's what's up, man," I said with a smile. "I could see it. I could see that happening for you. That drink you made—that was for real."

We shook on that and half-hugged.

"I'm gonna go get a little sleep," he said. "Maybe wake her up and get a little more action."

"Yeah, I'm gonna try to sleep a little too."

"You should wake Gabriela up," he said, shaking his head. "You see that ass?"

I smiled at that.

"See you in the morning," he said. "I'll make us some breakfast."

I nodded and he went back upstairs.

—

The living room was filled with sunshine by the time I woke up. I didn't want to bother Gabriela, so I slept in the chair next to the couch after smoking the blunt with Manny. I looked over to the couch and she was gone. Her clothes were gone too. I could still smell her though. I got up from the chair and felt dizzy. I rubbed my forehead and saw a note on the table next to my phone.

*Had fun last night. Hope u did too. If u ever wanna hook up or just hang out, call me. 347-555-9044 –G*

I folded the note and put it in my pocket. I checked my phone and it was nine o'clock. No new calls or texts from my mother. She was busy at her boyfriend's house.

I sat around for fifteen minutes until Manny and Maria came downstairs. They walked into the kitchen and I joined them there. Manny was wearing his outfit from the night before, but Maria was wearing a tight white T-shirt with no bra and some men's boxer shorts that were rolled up at the top. I could see her nipples through the shirt. Manny didn't care. She didn't care. No one did.

Manny looked past me and into the living room.

"Where's Gabriela?" he asked with a chin nod.

"I don't know," I said. "She rolled out."

He looked to Maria and she shrugged her shoulders. Maria didn't look like she was in the mood to talk, except to complain about a headache.

"Lemme make you a nice, Puerto Rican breakfast," he said. "So you can see how the kings eat."

"Sounds good, man," I said.

"Go chill in there, watch some TV, and I'll bring the food out when it's done."

"Cool," I said.

I went back into the living room and took a seat on the couch. I turned on the TV and flipped to ESPN. I could hear Manny and Maria in the kitchen, talking in Spanish. It sounded like they were having an argument. Check that, it sounded like Maria was doing all the arguing and Manny was just listening.

I turned the volume up a little louder on the TV.

My phone buzzed on the table. It was a text from my mother.

*Call me.*

I dialed her number and it rang twice before she picked up.

"Darnell," she said.

"Hey Mom."

"Don't 'Hey Mom' me," she snapped.

"Mom—"

"What the hell did you do?"

"I wasn't thinking and as soon as I knew it—"

"I need to see you at home right now."

"If you wanted to see me so bad, you would have been home after work," I said. "But you weren't there."

There was silence on the other end.

"I was home for a little bit to change clothes and you weren't there," I said.

"Boy, don't you turn this around on me," she said. "You screw up and then try to put it in on me?"

I didn't say anything.

She sighed.

"I'll be home in an hour," she said. "You better be too."

"Okay."

"Bye."

I hung up and put my phone back on the table. My head started pounding on both sides and I closed my eyes for a second. Just two days before, I was getting ready for the most important season of my life. And now . . .

Manny came in with a tray of food and he described all of the things that he made before allowing me to eat. He was definitely learning things at his restaurant job and I was happy for him. He really loved it. And it was good that he had a bigger purpose in this world than getting high and chasing ass.

I ate the delicious breakfast—Spanish sausage and Spanish *tortilla*—and helped him clean the kitchen and living room. After we finished, I checked my phone and saw that I had ten minutes to get home in time to meet my mother.

"I'm gonna bounce," I said.

"I'll roll one of the Black and Mild's and we can hit it before you go," Manny said with yellow dish gloves on. He was cleaning Maria's stove.

"Nah I'm good," I said. "No more weed until the summer. I gotta at least act like I'm still an athlete."

"Hey, good luck tomorrow, man," he said, taking off one of the gloves to give me a handshake. "I'm sure it'll go your way. And it was cool chillin', man—like old times."

"Thanks, man," I said. "*Muchas gracias* for everything."

"No doubt, D," he said. "No doubt."

I turned to Maria who was sitting on a stool and pouring coffee into a cup.

"Thank you for the hospitality," I said.

She waved half-heartedly and gave me an even weaker smile.

"Later," I said before turning to leave.

"Hey, D!" Manny said.

I turned back to look at him.

"Even if you are back on the team and you know, back at school," he said, "don't be a stranger. Come by the restaurant some time."

"That's a bet."

I turned back around, left the kitchen, and walked out of the house. That was night one of my party weekend. I stopped out in front of Maria's house and pulled out my phone. I scanned through Jessica's messages again and wondered whether or not I had the energy for a second night.

# TEN

I beat my mother home and there were no missed calls or messages from Coach on the answering machine. I lied down on the couch, put my feet up, and turned on the TV. It was noon. I couldn't remember the last time I had done that on a Saturday. Since as far back as I could remember, Saturdays during the school year were for sports and sports only. In the fall, it was football and in the spring, basketball. Middle school was when I made the decision to focus solely on basketball and left football behind.

I muted the TV and thought about my teammates. I wondered how the two practices went without me. Had they already moved on and left me behind? Had Coach named another captain to replace me? Even though it was only two days, I missed it—all of it. My teammates. Coach. Being in the locker room. Running up and down the court.

It was my team and I fucked it all up.

My phone buzzed and I sat up. It was a text from my mother.

*I got held up here. Where are you?*

*Home. Like u said.*

*Be there in another hour.*

I turned off the TV and got up from the couch. I went to my room and changed into some basketball shorts and a T-shirt. I threw on some running shoes and went downstairs for a run around the neighborhood. The temperature was that perfect mix of warmth with a little bit of chill underneath. The sun was out and people were too, enjoying their weekend. Whenever I had the free time—which was almost never—I loved to run around the neighborhood. And I could run all day too.

I started sweating instantly, though, faster than I would normally sweat during practice or a game. My body was trying to get rid of the poison that I was putting into it. I kept pushing through. I ran down Flatbush Avenue for three miles until I saw the outline of the bridge in the near distance. I stopped to stare at it for a minute. I had never jogged across the Brooklyn Bridge before, but I decided there was no better time than that moment to do it. I had all the time in the world.

I dashed toward the bridge with a burst of energy. The air got cooler as the ground elevated. My legs burned as I asked more of them, sprinting up the incline to the actual bridge.

There were lanes for bikers and joggers on the bridge. I ran to the halfway point and stopped to take a break. I looked back to Brooklyn and felt a love in my heart for the place that I came from. If it were my decision, I'd never leave. But the people around me—my mother, Coach—were always telling me that I had to leave Brooklyn to truly become a man.

I looked over to the other side at Manhattan, and I saw a strange place that I didn't know much about. Even though it was close—just a few blocks and across a bridge—I didn't have much experience being in Manhattan. My only experience being there came in the form of a few Friday movie nights with my mother and a handful of Knick games at Madison Square Garden.

I continued to the end of the bridge and right up to the line that separated the two boroughs. Manny's dream to open a restaurant in Manhattan crossed my mind and made me smile. With *how* we grew up and *where* we grew up, it would be something for a kid like Manny, a Brooklyn kid through and through, to show those people in Manhattan how to do it right.

Jessica lived in Manhattan too, and if I accepted her invitation, it would be my first experience there on my own without my mother or basketball to protect me.

I turned my back on Manhattan and ran back across the bridge to Brooklyn.

———

The run did me good. My body needed it and it took my mind away from basketball. I took a shower and had a seat on the couch again, waiting for my mother to walk in. A couple of the guys from the team texted me while I was out on my run. They asked me how I was and mentioned that Coach didn't say much about my absence and that they—the whole team—missed having me around. I replied that I thought that everything would work out, even though deep down inside I wasn't sure.

Jessica texted me again as well with what she called her "final offer." She said that if I wasn't coming over, she was going to go out with her friends and find someone else to fuck. Since she put it in those terms, the decision had been made for me. I would be heading to Manhattan that night.

*B there at eight*, I wrote.

*Perfect*, she wrote back.

My mother walked in the door just then and looked as if she had been up all night partying too. Her hair was puffed out in all different directions and her eyes were red. She did me a favor, coming home an hour after she said she would. The run allowed me to erase any trace that I had been drinking, smoking, and fucking the night before.

"Late night?" I asked.

"Staying up all night worrying about you," she said as she dropped her bag and keys on the table.

She walked into the kitchen. I got up off the couch and followed her.

"I'm fine," I said.

"Are you?"

"Yeah."

"Where were you all night?"

"Out with friends."

"Darnell, I'm not going to let you throw your whole future away," she said. "I'm not gonna do it."

"It'll be fine," I said. "Coach will take care of it."

"Oh really?" she asked. "This 'best player on the team' stuff will only take you so far. People get tired, Darnell. Tired of dealing with people's mistakes."

I didn't say anything.

"I don't want to even think about you getting expelled from school," she said.

"So let's not think about it."

She nodded. "Let's talk about what happened at the restaurant then."

I looked away from her.

"I've found a good man, Darnell," she said. "I know that you've had trouble with my boyfriends in the past."

"Trouble?" I asked. "That's what you think I had? Trouble?

"And a lot of them were no good," she said. "I know that."

I thought of one of them who would've been lucky to be described as "no good." My stomach began to churn like it was trying to swallow itself. That sickening feeling of hatred started to bubble and rise up into my throat.

"After a while, I stopped dating because I was afraid of how you would react," she said.

I opened my mouth. She didn't know. How could she?

No one did.

"Darnell, do you want to say something?"

The room spun and my face was covered in sweat. I dashed for the sink and made it just in time, throwing up all the liquor from the night before. Some of it came up through my nose and it stung as it came out of me.

"Darnell?" she said, grabbing the back of my shoulders. "What is it?"

It was all done. There was no more liquor to get out of my system. I couldn't tell her, though. I turned to look at her and there were tears in her eyes. I turned away because if I kept looking at her, I would start crying.

I turned the faucet on and put the nozzle to hot. I sprayed the water at the vomit and watched it trickle down the drain. My stomach turned over a couple more times.

"Sit down," she said. "Drink some water."

I took a seat at the table and she hurried over with a glass of water. I drank it slowly. After a little while, my breathing went back to normal and the dizziness was gone too.

"I just need to lie down," I said. "I'll be fine."

"Ok," she said. "Go lie down."

———

It was five in the afternoon when Jessica's texts woke me up in my bed. She sent me her address along with another description of what she was going to do to me that night. I didn't reply to her. I went into the kitchen to look for something to eat and there seemed to be even less to choose from than the day before. I had a bowl of cereal and a banana, my usual breakfast. As I tried to think about Jessica, Gabriela kept popping into my head. There was something good about her that I couldn't put my finger on. She was chill and sexy and all that, but there was more.

My mother walked into the kitchen and sat down at the table next to me. She was tired. Both of us were.

"I'm sorry there isn't anything in the fridge," she said. "I'll go shopping tomorrow."

"It's okay."

"Are you ready to talk?" she asked.

"There's nothing to talk about."

She put the back of her hand on my forehead.

"You're burning up," she said, getting up and going over to the sink. She soaked a rag in cold water and brought it back over to me at the table.

"Here," she said. "Hold this on your head."

"I need to go lie down again," I said, getting up from the table. "I'm going out tonight."

She put her hand out and grabbed onto mine.

"You're not going anywhere with a fever like this," she said.

I stared at her, holding the rag against my forehead.

"Okay," I said. "I'm just gonna chill. Go to bed early. Wait for Coach's call tomorrow."

She nodded and I walked back to my room.

━━━

I wasn't planning on lying to my mother about going to Jessica's house. I meant what I said. After the fever broke, I was really going to blow Jessica off and stay in the house. But when I woke up from another nap and saw that my mother had left—probably to her boyfriend's—that sealed it. Just because I told her I was in for the night didn't mean that she could leave and go spend time with her boyfriend.

I needed her too, now more than ever.

I had an hour and a half to burn and I opened my book bag to work on some schoolwork. Even though I wasn't sure I'd be at school on Monday, there was a lot of homework to do. I opened my math book to the problems, but it was no use. I couldn't focus. The schoolwork was intolerable without basketball.

There wasn't much to do at home. I was so used to being busy with basketball that I didn't know how to entertain myself there. I paced around for a little while, looked out the window, and watched the sun go down over Brooklyn. I thought about calling Gabriela, but for some reason, I texted Jessica that I was on my way instead.

I got ready and left the house shortly after. My fever broke and I felt almost normal. I caught a train into Manhattan. I put my headphones on and sat down at the front of a mostly empty car. The music helped take my mind off of the things that were going on. I nodded my head and mouthed the lyrics of the song.

The song was by one of my friends from the neighborhood. His rap name was Young Money—real name, Kenny Telfair—and we grew up together on the same block along with Manny and Mike. We used to call ourselves "The Bucktown Crew" and we made it our business to stay out late—as late as our mothers and grandmothers would allow—and run around with all the little freaks in neighborhood.

Things changed when basketball became it for me, though. I started seeing less of the guys in The Bucktown Crew—most of all, Kenny. I ran into him one time during the summer between junior and senior year. I hadn't seen him for three years before that. He had dropped out of school, just like many others, and was selling that stuff. Not weed or coke like Mike; he sold crack and heroin.

When we bumped into each other that day, he gave me one of his CDs for free and said that the drugs were just a way to keep his head up until his rap career hit. He also said that we needed to catch up and spend some more time like the old days. I told him he was right about that, but that was the last time I ever saw Kenny.

People were getting busted left and right in Brooklyn for possession of crack. The story goes that Kenny was so tired of being pressed by the cops in Brooklyn that he started selling up in Harlem. But he wasn't from Harlem, and that was a problem. Kenny took two to the chest and that was that. Young Money would have to live on through the songs saved on my phone and the memories of late summer days running around with The Bucktown Crew.

The train began stopping at different stations in Manhattan and that's when I started paying more attention to the stops than the music. Jessica lived in the Village near NYU and I was keeping my eyes open for the Eighth Street stop. After a few more minutes, the conductor called out "Eighth Street" as the next stop and I stood up from my seat. The train screeched to a hault and I mixed into a crowd of people on the platform.

I took the stairs from the platform and headed above ground. I continued down Broadway just like Jessica said to, and with some time to spare, I ducked into a pizza place to get a slice. I sat at the window eating my slice of pepperoni and watching the people walk by on Broadway. Manhattan had a different feel than Brooklyn. I could tell that from only a couple minutes being there.

Folks in Manhattan looked like they had places to be, and they looked like they were in a hurry to get there. People in Brooklyn weren't like that. We weren't in a rush to leave. We took our time with it. We wanted to be on those streets because we were those streets, and the streets were us.

I said a "thanks" in my head for Brooklyn as I finished my slice.

I continued down Broadway on the fifteen-minute walk to Jessica's place. I took my time.

When Jessica answered the door wearing nothing but her bra and underwear, I can't say that I was totally shocked. She made it pretty clear what she wanted, but I didn't want it to be that easy. I might've said that I wanted it that easy when I was bullshittin' with my boys, but deep down I wanted to work a little.

"Put some clothes on," I said. "I ain't that kind of dude. Let's hang out for a bit."

She frowned and let me inside. As I walked by her, I could smell her perfume—the sweet stuff again. I tried not to let it go to my head this time.

She went down the hall and quickly came back with jeans and a T-shirt on. I stood in what felt like the living room—with these big ass apartments, you could never really be sure which room is which. I stared out of a massive window that had a view of the park. With a little shift of the eyes, you could see the lights of Times Square blazing away. Somewhere back out there in the darkness was Brooklyn, but I didn't strain my eyes looking for it. I knew it was there.

"Was it hard to find?" she asked.

"Nah," I said.

She smiled and gave me a hug. I hugged her back, but didn't touch her ass.

"You want something to drink?" she asked. "A beer? Tequila?"

"Not right now," I said.

I stared at her, thinking on my plan to party hard for two straight days. It was a lot more fun hanging out with a group of people who are all having fun like the night before. Chilling with Manny was always the best. This with Jessica was different. It wasn't a party. I realized that one night of partying hard was probably enough.

"Sorry for hounding you," she said. "I just really wanted to be alone with you."

"It's cool."

We sat down on the couch that was in the huge room. She sat close to me.

"This place is off the hook," I said.

"Yeah, my dad does well," she said.

I smelled a little weed in the air. I sniffed at it like a dog.

"You been smoking weed?"

"I smoked a joint before you came," she said.

I smiled and shook my head. I'm not sure why I did. It didn't surprise me that she smoked. I just had a weird feeling going through me. I didn't really want to be there, but I also felt that I'd be missing something if didn't show up.

"You seem confused," she said.

I didn't tell her that she was right.

"You want me to roll another one?" she asked in a hopeful voice.

"I'm good," I said. "I got lit last night. I probably need to cool out a little."

She nodded with understanding, but couldn't hide the disappointment on her face.

"Will you be back at school on Monday?" she asked.

I shrugged.

"I told you about the crazy rumors floating around at school."

"Yeah."

"What happened?" she asked.

"Something that shouldn't have happened," I said. "But whatever you're hearing at school is worse than what really happened."

"So why can't you tell me *what* happened?"

"It's not important," I said. "The important thing is if I'm allowed to walk through those halls again on Monday. And if Coach let's me back on the floor. That's really it."

"Whatever happened," she said, "I'm sure they're not gonna kick you out of school. You're the best player on the team and the school needs you."

"Everybody thinks that," I shot back. "But Coach doesn't play that. He's doesn't want to just win above everything else. He's always in my ear about life and shit—a lot more lately. He's always talking about how basketball can't be the only thing that defines me. I feel like he could kick me off the team just to prove a point or some shit."

She stared at me, blinking her eyes.

"He named me Captain too," I said before shaking my head. "I really let him down. I could see it on his face."

I saw the bored look on her face. I waved my hand at the air.

"Whatever," I said.

She popped up off the couch.

"We need to change the mood in here," she said.

She went to the entertainment center across from the couch and pressed a button on the tuner. There was an iPod connected to it and it lit up blue when the tuner came alive. She scrolled through the music and picked a song. It was one of those rap songs that you hear all day on the radio. I couldn't stand a lot of what was on the radio, but she liked it and I didn't want to complain.

She came back over to the couch and started dancing in front of me. She turned around to show me her hips and ass. It was her ass that made her dangerous. Everything else—breasts, face, personality—was just okay. But she had ass for days, and that made her a factor.

She moved closer to me, still dancing, until finally she jumped into my lap. I could feel the weight of her butt while she moved it back and forth over my dick. It got hard with the quickness and she felt it moving underneath her. The "evil" was back to take control of me. It didn't even need alcohol or weed this time.

She felt me with her hand and I brought her in close for a kiss. She opened her mouth and stuck her tongue halfway down my throat. I needed some air after a few seconds of that. I kissed her all over her neck, and the sweetness of her scent flooded my nose and matched the taste of lips. Her eyes narrowed and she licked her honey-scented lip-gloss. She went in for another kiss.

The room suddenly became hot—too hot—and I tossed her off of me onto the couch. She landed with a light thud and she stared at me in shock like I had violated her.

I stood up from the couch and walked over to turn the music off.

"What's going on?" she asked.

"I don't know. This doesn't seem right."

"Right?"

"Yeah."

"*What* doesn't feel right?" she asked.

"What do you get out of it?"

"Get out of *it*?" she said, her voice almost at its cracking point. "I really like you."

"You don't know shit about me," I said. "We don't come from the same place."

She stared at me again in shock.

"Did you think that we were actually gonna be together?" I asked. "Like, *be* together?"

"I didn't think . . . " she said before stopping. "I

just thought we were going to have some fun. And then go from there."

"You probably just wanted to fuck the star basketball player," I said. "The black, big-dick, star basketball player. I don't know why. Maybe to show off for your friends? Maybe to piss your dad off?"

"That's fucked up," she said.

I didn't say anything to that.

"Why did you show up then?" she asked with the beginnings of anger in her voice. "Why did you even come to my house?"

I shook my head and then looked down to the floor. I took a deep breath and felt her staring at me. I looked up and my eyes met hers.

"Truth?" I asked.

She nodded and her eyes were glistening—tears would be coming soon.

"I want to do it," I said. "I wanted to do it. I wanted to fuck you. I mean you're fine. You're rich. And you're down."

A tear slid down her cheek.

"But mostly I wanted to come here and figure out the reason why I shouldn't do it," I said.

We stood together silent for a moment.

She opened her mouth and yelled for me to get out of her house. She pointed toward the door and repeated for me to do so several times. One time was enough for me and as I made my way out, I could hear her following me to the door. When I got to it and opened it, I turned around and saw that her face was covered in tears.

Then she slammed the door shut at my back. The hallway was dead silent.

I got out of her building as quick as I could and started walking down the street, looking for the first subway station I could find. It was a stupid decision, coming to Manhattan in the first place. I should have known; I should have thought first and figured out that nothing good was going to come of it, just like trying to cross the street in front of school without using the intersection.

But I was making a lot of stupid decisions those

days. And this was supposed to be a big year for me. This was supposed to be the year I put it all together.

Things were falling apart, and it felt like I couldn't do anything to stop it.

I found a train station and hopped on the first train I saw, not even paying attention to where it was going. When I took my seat, I put my head in my hands.

"This shit could come back to bite me," I whispered to myself. "Fuck. This could be bad."

That was all I needed at school. More rumors. I prayed that Jessica wasn't the type to show up at school on Monday, crying tears of anger, telling the principal that the once star basketball player had sexually assaulted her or some shit.

# ELEVEN

I got home after a few wrong turns on the subway. It was ten thirty when I sat down on the couch in my living room. My thoughts were racing. I thought for sure that Jessica was gonna burn me. Yeah, it was fucked up what I did to her. I should've just told her from the start that I wasn't interested. But like I told her, I felt that I was justified. It made sense in my head. Jessica obviously didn't see it that way.

There were a bunch of bad scenarios playing out in my head. I couldn't see what my future held and that scared the shit out of me. With all the partying I'd done through my high school years, with all the different girls I had been with, I had always avoided that major mistake. Even though I didn't do anything to Jessica, even though we didn't have sex, this felt like one of those mistakes.

A rumor of a sexual nature at school was all that was needed to crush my hopes of college scholarship. That could send things over the edge. It didn't matter that nothing actually happened between the two of us. It's what people think happened. I was on thin ice already. A rumor like that would break the ice.

I picked up my phone from the coffee table and texted Jessica.

*Hi,* I wrote. *Can we talk?*

It took her ten minutes to respond before she wrote back, *Talk about what???*

*What happened?*

Another five minutes passed before she wrote back, *That was 2 messed up . . . I don't even kno what to say 2 u right now.*

*We cool?*

She wrote back quickly: *Cool?*

*Yea. Ur not gonna tell anybody that some foul shit went down between us right?*

*Foul shit? Like what?*

This time I paused. I wanted to make sure I wrote the right thing. I tried writing it a bunch of different ways but it didn't look right on my phone. I finally wrote it in the simplest way I could, the way that made the most sense.

*Like u tellin people that I raped you or something like that. Ur not gonna go wild on me like that, right?*

I pressed "Send."

She didn't respond for fifteen minutes or so. My whole future rested on the reply that she was going to send back to me. I waited for my phone to buzz and fought the urge to hound her with more texts, demanding an answer right away. But growing up with a single mother taught me how to give a woman space. I had to thank my mother for that lesson. Pushing Jessica for a response could've hurt my cause.

My phone buzzed finally. I looked down at the text and read it a few times.

*I won't do that 2 u. As much as it would surprise u 2 kno, I'm not nasty like that. But if u are allowed back at school, when we c each other around, don't say shit 2 me. Don't look at me. We're dead 2 each other. Got it?*

*Got it*, I wrote. *Sorry about this fucked up night.*

She didn't reply to that. The two of us never exchanged texts or spoke to one another in person again.

# TWELVE

I went into my room and put my head down on my pillow. I dodged one bullet. Sunday would be the day that I would find out if I dodged another one—the big one. There was something else weighing on me though: the thing with my mother and her new boyfriend. I had to deal with it somehow, even though every part of me wanted to avoid it.

Why would she bring this shit up now?

With all the shit going on in my life, with how important this year was for me, I didn't need my own mother adding to it.

Why did she have to go and get herself a boy-friend?

My eyelids were wide open as I tried to shut the thoughts down. It was no use. I didn't have anybody to talk to, but desperately needed to get something out. I sat up in bed and took a sheet of paper and a pen from out of my book bag. I turned on the light and sat down at the desk in the corner of my room.

I started writing a letter.

———

*Dear Gabriela,*

*I'm eight years old again in that place I've always known. That old Brooklyn neighborhood, where, even though you knew everyone, safety wasn't promised. The neighborhood was a much louder place back then. There was a lot more drama too. It's hazy, but if I think back hard enough, the memories, good and bad, come back like it was yesterday.*

*I saw my share of violence around the old neighborhood. I saw cops, white and black, not giving a* shit. Most of the cops were more interested in getting blowjobs from the hookers working Avenue U and Flatbush than fighting crime. That's what older guys hanging out in the neighborhood used to say, anyway.

My mother protected me from everything. She didn't want the streets getting hold of me. So I wasn't allowed to be outside, hanging out on the block. And if I did manage to sneak out when she was at work, she would find out when she got home. She knew. She could see the streets written all over my face. She would try to explain to me that I didn't belong out there, that I could be something more, that she would make sure that I became something more. I didn't understand then. But I loved my mother. I knew that. And more than anything, I didn't want to disappoint her.

She didn't want me to be angry about not having my father around. She protected me from that too. That's where basketball came in. That's where coaches came in. I guess she thought that basketball could help her raise me. And she was right about that. Without basketball, I don't know where I would be.

But as strong as she was, she couldn't protect me from this. And I don't blame her for it. I'm not mad at her for it. It just happened. And I'm the one who has to deal with it.

I was nine. It was summertime and that good feeling was all around me. I didn't have school to worry about. During the days, I went to a basketball camp in the Bronx that my mother had to work overtime to pay for. And when camp was over for the day, she would pick me up and we would take the train together back to Brooklyn. It was one of the happiest times of my life—basketball during the day, spending time with my mother at night.

Things changed halfway through the summer, though. This man started coming with her to pick me up from camp. He was her new "friend." I didn't like him the first time I saw him. I couldn't understand why my mother liked him or what she saw in him.

Things got worse. Shortly thereafter, he moved

in with us. He fucked everything up. He fucked my perfect summer up.

I never told anyone about this. No one else knows. But one time, when my mother was at work and I had a day off from camp, it was just the two of us there, me and her new "friend." He didn't work or was in between jobs, one of the two.

He was a drinker. The kind of person who was out on the corner. The kind of person that my mother did not want me to become. Why would she be attracted to that? Why would she let that into our home?

I still don't understand why.

I can't understand why.

He drank a lot that day. I could see the beer cans lined up in the kitchen when I went in there to get some juice or cereal or whatever. He stared at me while I was in the kitchen. The stare was angry, like I had done something to him. I hurried back to my room and shut the door.

Then I heard the footsteps coming toward my door. They were stumbling, heavy steps. I locked my door and hid in my closet. And I remember thinking that I wanted to be somewhere else, anywhere but there. And that I missed my mother. And that something bad was going to happen to me.

*Why would she let that into our house?*

Something bad did happen to me. He opened my door by putting a shoulder into it. I held my breath and he walked into my room. He paused. I could see him through the slit in the closet door. And then he walked over to the closet. He called out my name. I could smell the beer on his breath through the door. And if I try hard enough, I can still smell it to this day. He opened the door and looked down at me with a blank face. That was the worst part of it. He didn't look mean or scary or anything like that. He looked like he had done something like this before. He grabbed me by the arm and no matter how hard I tried to resist, I couldn't overcome the fact that he was a man and I was a boy.

He walked me over to my bed and sat me down next to him. He took his thing out and made me touch it. The tears streamed down my face at that point, and they didn't stop coming until it was over. No matter what the act was, whether I did something to him or the opposite, the tears streamed down my face. It hurt at the beginning, when he put it in, until it didn't anymore.

And after it was over, I was never the same. The pain came back. And it would stay with me.

I wasn't a little boy anymore. I was a man.

My mother's new "friend" stopped staying at our house after that day. It was some time at the end of the summer where her "friend" stopped coming around altogether—he never came with my mother to pick me up from camp anymore.

I was a different person after that day.

And you are the first person to ever know about this.

- D

---

I finished the letter and the thought of sleep wasn't even a possibility. I found the piece of paper with

Gabriela's number on it. I took a chance. There was something good about her other than the way she looked.

I knew it.

I took a chance.

I texted her.

She was awake and texted me back right away.

She said she would come over. She asked me to give her an hour. She would find her way over to my neighborhood from Fort Green.

# THIRTEEN

Gabriela was right on time. Even though it was late at night, she looked beautiful.

"Hi," she said simply when I met her in front of my building.

We walked side by side to the door of my apartment and went in.

We sat down on the couch in the living room. She put her bag down on the coffee table.

"What do you want to talk about?" she asked.

I handed her the letter.

"Read that," I said. "Then we'll talk."

She began to read it. I walked out of the living room and went into my room. I went over to my window and looked out of it. The city was still awake. There was a lot going on out there. I was miles and miles away from it all though. There was a distance growing between my city and me. It hit me right there. If I was allowed back at school and back on the team, and if things went the way they were supposed to go with the season and the scholarship offers were there, I had to leave Brooklyn.

"Darnell!" Gabriela called out to me from the living room.

I walked into the living room and sat down on the couch next to her.

"This is heavy," she said.

"Yeah."

"Why did you give it to me?" she asked. "We barely know each other."

"I don't know," I said. "I had to tell someone. And I felt something with you the other night. Something good."

She smiled, but didn't say anything.

"And things have been happening lately," I said.

"With my mother and then at school. It was gonna come out of me soon. I could feel it."

"Do you feel better?"

"I'm glad you're here, if that's what you're asking," I said. "But I'm not sure if it's gonna help or not."

"You never said anything to your mom?" she asked.

I shook my head.

"Why not?"

"Her life was hard enough. She was lonely a lot of the time. I remember that. And when this guy left the picture," I said, nodding to the letter still in her hand, "she cried every night for probably two weeks. I could hear her from my room. She thought I was asleep. Or maybe she didn't. I don't know for sure."

Gabriela stared at me.

"I felt guilty," I said. "I felt responsible for them not being together anymore."

"You should tell her now," she said.

"I think it was important for me to tell some-one," I said. "But I'm not sure if it's important that I tell her. It might crush her."

"She needs to know."

"I'm not sure yet," I said. "She's been trying to get me to talk since she told me about her new boyfriend, but I haven't been able to."

"Did you hear from your coach yet?" she asked with a little smile. "About whether or not you're still a superstar?"

I shook my head and smiled back.

"Tomorrow."

We sat quiet on the couch for a few minutes. It wasn't uncomfortable at all though. It was the opposite.

"Do you think it's weird?" I asked. "What hap-pened to me?"

Her eyes went away from mine for a second and then came back.

"That you were molested?"

"Yeah," I said.

"It's not weird," she said. "You were a kid. That shit happens. It's fucked up, but you ain't the only one in the world it happened to."

"Is it gonna be with me forever?"

"I don't think so," she said.

"You think I'll be able to get past it?"

"I don't know," she said before pausing to think. "But I'll help you if you want," she said. "I'll be here for you."

I smiled and looked away before the tears started. I looked back at her and there was no danger of the tears coming now. I stopped them.

"I've never been able to talk to a girl like I can talk to you."

She smiled.

"Did you feel something with me the other night?" I asked. "The same thing I felt with you?"

She looked right into my eyes without blinking.

"Yes," she said.

And now her eyes were starting to water.

"I like you," I said.

"I like you too."

"Can you stay here tonight?" I asked. "We don't have to do anything. I just want you here with me."

"Yes," she said.

We went to my room and got into bed. We didn't have sex. She fell asleep in my arms. She slept comfortably there throughout the night. I didn't sleep much. I watched over her mostly. I focused on the sound of her soft breathing. It was one of the best sleeps I'd ever had.

# FOURTEEN

**W**e woke up early the next morning. Gabriela left before my mother got home because she wanted us to have our talk. She told me again to come clean. I told her again that I would think about it. She gave me a kiss at the door. I told her that I wanted us to be together and she said that she wanted that too. She also said again that she would try to help me get over my past.

I walked her down to the subway station because I wanted every moment I could get with her.

I kissed her one last time before she went underground.

I walked back home and my mother wasn't there yet.

No call from Coach yet either.

It was nine thirty when my mother arrived. She called my name when she entered and I walked into the living room to greet her. She looked refreshed and happy. Normally on Sundays, she was grumpy and tired from the long workweek prior and the one that was about to come.

Like I said before, things were changing.

She put the back of her hand to my forehead.

"Your fever's gone," she said with a smile.

"I feel better," I said.

"Well give me a hug," she said.

I stepped into her arms and she wrapped them around me as tight as she could. She sighed as she pulled me close and I leaned my face down into hers. She gave me a kiss on the cheek.

We pulled away from each other and she looked down to the floor.

"I didn't want to wake you yesterday while you were resting," she said.

"It's okay, Mom," I said.

I didn't tell her that I needed her there with me yesterday. It was okay now that I had Gabriela.

"Really," I said. "It's okay."

She smiled and reached up to touch my face.

"You want some breakfast?"

"Yeah."

The sizzle of eggs in a frying pan filled the kitchen with both a pleasant sound and smell. Even though to me it looked like we had very little in the fridge, she created a feast for us. It was always like that with her. She performed magic in the kitchen and made the most of what we had. I realized right there that she was a success.

I had to be a success as well, no matter how the incident at school turned out.

I had to go to college, with or without a basketball scholarship. I owed it to her.

I owed it to myself.

"Yesterday, you looked like you needed an entire day in bed," she said with her back to me, pulling slices of bread out of the toaster. "Is that what you did? Sleep the whole time?"

"Pretty much," I said.

She gave me an uncertain look. "Okay."

"What about you?" I asked. "How was your night?"

"It was fine."

She filled my plate and then her own, and we began eating. We didn't talk for a little while, even though we both knew that we had things to talk about.

I think the silence got to her after a while. She stopped eating after a couple of bites, then picked at her food a little before finally dropping the fork out of her hand and onto her plate.

She sighed.

"He's a good man, Darnell," she said. "His name is Milton and he's a lawyer. He treats me with respect and he loves me. I've never felt that from a man before, other than you." She smiled. "And I don't want to stop feeling it."

I nodded.

"Can you understand that?"

Telling her, after all these years, about what happened to me that day in the summer would only hurt her future. That's the only thing it would do. It would not change things. My mother would blame herself. I knew her. We were alike in that way. She wouldn't be able to let it go.

"Yeah, Mom," I said. "I just want you to be happy."

The look of concern on her face turned into a smile. It was the most beautiful smile I had ever seen on her face.

"I'm glad you're happy," I said.

"Thank you."

I couldn't do it. I couldn't crush her. She didn't deserve that.

And besides, I had Gabriela now. She would be there behind me to help me deal with my past. I wasn't sure if that was enough or if I was strong enough to overcome it, but I had to try.

"I'm gonna go to the market after breakfast," she said, "and fill up this fridge. I'll make you something special for dinner. What do you want?"

"Let's go out," I said. "Dinner and movie."

She smiled. "It's a date."

As I helped clean up breakfast, I thought about Manny cleaning up at Maria's that morning and then the luck that brought Gabriela into my arms. All of it made me shake my head a few times, but it also made me understand just how fortunate I was.

If it wasn't for my mother telling me about her new boyfriend, I wouldn't have jet out of the diner and gotten home so late. If I wasn't late getting home, I wouldn't have overslept the next morning. If it wasn't for me oversleeping the next morning, I wouldn't have had the accident in front of school. And if it wasn't for the accident in front of school, I would've never been sent home, and the party at Maria's house would've never happened. Well, knowing Manny, the party would've still happened. I just wouldn't have been there.

I put the orange juice away and closed the refrigerator door. My mother was taking a sponge to the counter to get all of the loose crumbs and stains.

"Manny," I said underneath my breath. "Goddamn if it wasn't for Manny."

"What?" she asked as she finished wiping down the counter.

"Nothing," I said.

———

My mother was out at the market when the nerves started to kick in. I was ready for Coach's call. I wanted him to call while she was out. Good news or bad, it would be easier to take the call if she wasn't around.

The house phone rang a couple of times. One of

the calls was from my aunt and the second call was from someone who had dialed a wrong number.

My phone buzzed with a text. It was Gabriela.

*Did u talk to ur mom?*

*Not really. I couldn't.*

*Ok. Hear from ur coach?*

*No.*

*I'm sure it will work out.*

*I'll let you know as soon as I hear.*

*Ok.*

*Can't wait 2 c u again.*

*Me too :)*

As soon as I put my phone down on the coffee table, it rang. It was Coach. I took a deep breath and answered.

"Hello, Coach," I said.

"Darnell," he said on the other end. His voice was tired. It seemed like everyone connected to me was tired right about then.

"What's up, Coach?" I asked.

"I've been talking to the administrators at

school, along with the principal, since Friday after the incident."

"Give it to me, Coach," I said. "I'm ready to deal with it."

"We've decided to allow you to come back to school," he said. "And you are allowed to stay on the team."

There was silence.

"You there, Darnell?" he asked after a few moments.

A couple of tears ran down my face, but I made sure not to let him know I was crying.

"Yeah, Coach," I said.

"This was not an easy decision," he said. "The school is going to have to pay out some money for the accident."

"I'm sorry, Coach—"

"Don't apologize anymore, Darnell," he said. "I think you know that this is your last chance. No more apologies."

"I know," I said.

"That's not all," he said. "You have to do fifty hours of community service from now until the end of the school year."

"I'm just curious, Coach," I said. "Did the city say I have to do community service? Or the school?"

"Let's just say that it was a collective decision," he said. "The cops, the city, and the school."

"Got it."

"Even though you're busy with basketball, you have to make the time to fulfill this obligation. Off days, weekends, whatever."

"Okay, Coach."

"Come to my office before school tomorrow," he said. "Be-fore school. That means thirty minutes before. I have your missed school assignments from Friday and there's more to talk about in person."

"I'll be there on time."

"I bet you had a rough weekend with your mother," he said. "She'd kill you if you got yourself thrown out of school."

"I learned a lot this weekend, Coach."

"Good," he said. "Let's see if you can put any of it to use."

I didn't say anything to that.

"Thirty minutes before school, Darnell," he said. "See you then."

"See you then, Coach."

"Okay."

"And Coach," I said quickly before he hung up, "thank you."

"Don't thank me," he said. "I'm just trying to teach you something here."

"Bye, Coach."

# FIFTEEN

You best believe I was up early the next morning. It was so early that *I* woke my mother up. I made breakfast for her—a simple hardboiled egg and toast along with coffee—and when she walked into the kitchen and saw it all laid on the kitchen table, she asked me if it was Mother's Day. I told her no, that I just wanted to say thanks.

As I walked to the train station, the early morning workers were getting started with their jobs. They swept in front of their stores and they took the trash out from the night before. It was too early to talk. Everyone around the neighborhood knew that. A simple nod would do. That passed for early morning hospitality in Brooklyn.

It was warm for late October. It reminded me of the summer days—Manny knocking on my door early on Saturday mornings. We'd be out all day at the pool or on the basketball courts. And as soon as the sun started to drop, I'd be on my way home—because that was my mother's rule—while Manny and the rest of the guys would stay out for the rest of the night, chilling in the cool night air.

The train was right on time and I got to school a whole fifteen minutes before Coach asked me to be there. That was progress. But the question of commitment would always hang over me. Would I stay committed to basketball? Would I be committed to college if basketball got me there? Would I be committed to a girl for the first time? Most importantly, would I stay committed to life?

Life used to be cheap where I lived. The cost of it had raised a little as the years passed, but old habits were hard to break.

I dropped off some books at my locker and grabbed the books that I needed for my classes before lunch. I went through the locker room and a strange feeling washed over me. My two-day absence from the team felt like much longer. The place where I spent countless hours now felt like a foreign country. I continued on to Coach's office. I checked my phone right outside his closed door. Five minutes early.

I knocked and he told me to come in.

I went inside and he stared at me blankly. He waved a hand to sit down in front of him.

I sat.

"Early," he said.

I nodded.

"Your letters came in on Friday," he said. "After I sent you home."

He tossed a pile of about five letters over to me. They dropped onto the desk with a slap.

"Those five schools are going to offer you a full ride," he said.

I took the letters in my hand and held them tight.

"We'll talk about them," he said. "Later."

"Okay Coach," I said.

We sat there silent for a moment. It was early. We *were* in Brooklyn.

"It used to scare me to even think of leaving Brooklyn," I said.

Coach smiled. "You gotta learn to be on time before you can think of leaving Brooklyn."

"I know," I said. "I know. I'm trying to work on that. And a few other things."

"I'm glad to hear that, Darnell."

"Is there anything we need to talk about?"

"No more talk, Darnell," he said. "Just wanted to give those to you."

I put the letters into my book bag.

"Go on to class," he said. "You owe me some sprints today at practice too." He chuckled to himself. "And about thirty-five points per game this season."

"I got you on the sprints," I said as I stood up from the chair and hung the strap of my book bag over a shoulder. "As for the thirty-five points a game, I'll try my best on that."

"We have a rough schedule this year," he said.

"I know."

"The roughest and the baddest, Darnell," he said.

"How we like it," I said.

He smiled one last time as I left his office and went to first period.

———

During my senior year, we finished that murderous regular season schedule of ours with a record of thirty-three and one. I was named most outstanding player of our section's playoffs and we easily won all of our games there pushing our record to thirty-seven and one. In the city championship game we got a chance for revenge against the one team that did beat us during the regular season. The game we lost came during mid-season at the hands of the best team in the Catholic league. They beat us at their place by three points with the help of some shaky calls from the refs. I didn't have a very good game; it was my worst of the season by far. I forced shots, got into early foul trouble, and turned the ball over nine times.

The site for the city championship game was neutral: Madison Square Garden. I can't tell you how sick it was playing at the Garden. For real. Even the referees couldn't protect the other team from the early scoring barrage that I put on them. I had the first ten points of the game, and not just for my team; we started out the game on a ten to nothing run. After they called a timeout to slow us down, the game took on more of a normal flow with each team more or less trading baskets. We were up twenty-nine to twenty-one after the first quarter and I had sixteen points.

In the second quarter, they made an adjustment

on me. They trapped aggressively anytime I touched the ball over half-court and some of their coverages I had never seen before. They ended up going on a ten-to-nothing run of their own to take the lead by one point.

After two straight bad passes by me, Coach called a timeout. The starters took seats on the bench and Coach sat on a little stool in front of us.

"Okay, take a deep breath," he said. "It's fine."

We all took deep breaths, even the guys who weren't in the game.

"It's not supposed to be easy," he said. "But you guys know that already. You guys are all tough guys, Brooklyn guys."

He jabbed a thumb across the way at the other team.

"But they are too," he said. "That's what this is about. Remember, at the beginning of the year, what I told you guys?"

He looked around at the huddle.

"I told you that I wanted you to learn something

this year," he said. "Something about yourselves. Something about the world."

The buzzer sounded and the starters stood up.

Coach put his hand in front of me before I walked onto the court.

"I want you to take a breather, Darnell," he said.

"What?"

"Just sit next to me," he said. "Just for a couple of minutes. I want you to see from the sidelines how they're defending you."

I didn't say anything. I just wanted to go back in that game.

"Two minutes," he said. "These are gonna be the most important two minutes of the game for you, so pay attention."

I took a seat next to Coach and the game started back up without me. I was upset, but I didn't complain. Instead, I focused my attention to the action on the court. I saw that other team's defense was very strong. Once they withstood my early scoring barrage, they settled in and rattled me with their traps.

Coach didn't say anything to me as I sat there on the bench next to him. I noticed that the other team was really good at overloading their defense on the strong side. They were also smart angles. That's why their traps worked well. There had to be a way to attack them once their defense settled on the strong side.

I couldn't see it at first. Then I thought back to that first practice of the season where Coach made us pass the ball five times before attacking on offense. Could that have been it? Did Coach make us play that way in the scrimmage at the end of the first practice of the season just to get us ready for something like this?

I looked over to Coach.

"I'm ready," I said.

He eyed me and then nodded.

"Next dead ball," he said.

I nodded and ran down to the scores table. I

looked up at the ceiling of the Garden as I waited to check into the game. The other team had extended their lead to five with me off the floor, but there were still five minutes left to go in the half. It was plenty of time to take the momentum back, plenty of time for me to do damage.

Plenty of time for *us* to do damage.

I checked back into the game after a shooting foul on us. As the player waited to take his shots, I quickly gathered the guys up in a little huddle right under the basket.

"Remember the first practice of the season?" I yelled over the roar of the crowd in the packed lower bowl of the Garden. "The scrimmage?"

"You mean how we had to pass five times first before taking a shot?" Leonard asked.

"Yeah," I said. "That's what we're gonna do right now."

My other four teammates looked at me like I had lost it.

"The shit'll work," I said.

They went with it, even though they didn't really believe me. But we didn't have much choice. The other team was starting to take control with their suffocating defense and our fast start in the first quarter was becoming a distant memory.

I brought the ball up the floor with us down seven after the free throws. They didn't come with their aggressive traps, but they were still ready to overload the strong side. I had the ball at the top of the key on the right and quickly swung it to Tramon on the left side. He swung it back to me without a single dribble and then I swung the ball to a teammate in the right corner. Their defense was moving now, unable to set a wall like they had been doing, and on the fifth pass, Leonard had deep post position on the right block and went up for an easy shot and two points. Five passes got us a score. We were down five.

After a stop, I took the ball and brought it up the court again, looking for the quick swing passes. Going at it like that created these little gaps in the defense that weren't there if we simply tried to attack with the dribble or force-feed it down low to Leonard.

After the third pass, I got the ball back at the left elbow and saw the weak side was wide open. I faked a pass back to the top of the key where Tramon was and instead threw a skip pass to my teammate in the corner. That made their whole defense react, and once again, Leonard had deep post position and took the fifth pass for an easy lay-in. Five passes and another score. We were down by three now with three minutes to go in the half.

They hit a three on their next possession to push the lead back up to six and we finished the half with scores on every possession but two using the five-pass strategy. The only problem to end the half was our defense. They scored on half of their remaining possessions, leaving them up by three going into the locker room.

I was stuck on sixteen points at the half, but

I had five assists *and* I figured out how to attack their defense.

The locker room felt calm at the half, even though we blew a big lead from the first quarter.

"This team that you guys are playing represents the challenge I talked about at the beginning of the season," Coach said. "Losing to them during the season was probably the best thing that could've happened for us. You guys needed to be humbled. Things were coming too easy for you."

Everyone was looking up at Coach as he spoke, even his assistants.

"Same thing at the beginning of this game," he said. "You jump out to a big a lead and you think it's over."

He paused and smiled.

"That's life," he said. "There's a resiliency that you gotta have to play this game. And that's what I love about it. Basketball is a lot like life. Things happen to you during the course of a game. Some things you can control, some you can't. But you gotta keep going out there and get in your defensive stance. Ready for whatever is gonna come at you next. You gotta love the burn."

Coach's eyes met mine. He smiled at me.

"It's life, guys."

When the third quarter started, we picked up our defensive intensity and really *that's* where the game changed again.

We all used our speed and long arms to get into the passing lanes, which led to steals that ended in fast-break scores. There was no need to pass the ball five times when we were getting easy layups and dunks. We were up six now. I had it at the top of the key and they decided that it was time to use their traps again. I was ready for them now; instead of trying to split the traps myself like in the first half, I quickly moved the ball to an open teammate, who then found another teammate for a layup or open three.

We busted the game wide open, taking a twenty-one-point lead at the end of the third quarter.

Coach took me off the ball in the middle of the third and I was able to get my offense going again with twelve straight points, and twenty by the end of the quarter. We were still breaking down their traps with ball movement; the only difference was that I was not handling the ball. I was finishing plays instead of making them.

Coach took me out at the end of the third and I wouldn't play another minute in the game. I finished with thirty-six points, eleven assists, four rebounds, and nine steals.

"Sit next to me, Darnell," Coach said after he pulled the starters out and put five bench players out on the court.

I sat down next to him on the bench. Our reserves were just as effective as the starters were at using the defense to ignite fast breaks and using the five-pass strategy to stretch the other team's defense.

"Why didn't you say something about using five passes on offense during the game we lost to them?" I asked, nodding to court. "We could've had a perfect season."

"Life's not perfect, Darnell."

I knew what he meant.

"And besides, I said it before, and I'm going to say it again," he said, "I wanted you guys to learn something this season."

I looked up in the Garden stands and tried to find my mother and Gabriela. I couldn't find them. It was okay though. They'd be waiting for me after the game.

"You did," he said. "You learned something. You might not know what it is right now. But you did. I saw it."

"I didn't think I was gonna make it for a while," I said.

Coach patted me on the back as we watched the reserves take it to the team who gave us our only loss of the season. As the seconds ticked away, the lower bowl of the Garden started to thin out a bit as our fans took over with chants and songs. I couldn't help but get emotional. I had come a long way from the beginning of the season. The unexpected crisis actually helped me get to that point. I patted Coach on the back and walked down to the end of the bench. I wanted to enjoy the last few minutes of the game with my teammates.

The final buzzer sounded and confetti dropped down onto the court. Coach was the first person I hugged.

"Just day by day," he said into my ear. "Keep doing things the right way, day in and day out, and see where you end up. My guess is you'll make it all the way to the league, D. I believe in you."

"Thanks, Coach."

When it was time for us to cut the nets down, the Garden was almost empty, save for players, coaches, and close family members. My mother, Gabriela, and Milton were on the floor to join in the celebration. The last three strands to be cut down were saved for the three captains of the team. The three seniors—Tramon, Leonard, and me. Tramon went up the ladder first and snipped his piece of the net off. He was off to Baylor on a scholarship in the fall. I gave him a big hug before he went over to join his mom, dad, and little brother. Leonard went up next and got his piece of the net. When he got down, he handed me the scissors before giving me a hug. Leonard hadn't decided on his school yet. And even though it was pretty late in the process, there was still time. He, like me, was raised by a single mother, and he met her at midcourt where they shared a moment.

I went up the ladder to get my piece of the net. I cut the last strand that connected the net to the rim. After putting my piece of the net into the buckle of my backwards city championship hat, I wore the net around my neck.

I took a deep breath before going down the ladder and stepping onto the floor.

We finished the season with a record of thirty-eight and one. We won the city championship by twenty points, destroying the team who gave us our only loss of the season, and I was named most valuable player of the game.

The thing that I'm most proud to say, though, is that I wasn't late for a single practice or class during the rest of the school year. Nobody was ever gonna call me lazy again.

———

I chose to attend the University of Maryland the following fall. They offered me a full athletic scholarship and a spot in the starting lineup. They were the only school of the five that made me offers that told me I would start right off the bat. That was a no-brainer for me. We don't come off the bench in Brooklyn.

It wasn't as hard as I thought it was going to be to leave Brooklyn after all those years. I *had* to do it. The bigger problem was leaving my mother and Gabriela. The rest of it—the neighborhood, my boys, pick-up games in the park, the feeling you get walking down Flatbush on a hot, summer day—those things could live on in my memories.

Gabriela wasn't upset that I left. She took the bus down from NYC to D.C. for visits once or twice a month. She knew it was best for me to leave. And whenever I called her late at night, telling her that I missed Brooklyn to death and that I missed her to death, or that I couldn't handle *it*, she was there to talk me off that ledge.

I loved her for that.

Things with my mother got better too. I met her boyfriend, Milton, around Christmas time of my senior year in high school and she was right; he was a good man. Meeting him didn't affect me at all. He was just a person. He was a man who liked my mother. It took me a long time—almost ten years—to realize that not all males who liked my mother were the same as the one from that summer day, years back.

When the following fall came and it was time to go to Maryland, my mother rented a car and we drove up there together. Her and Milton helped me move into to my first dorm room—the first dorm room ever used by someone in our family because I was the first to go to college. When they got back to Brooklyn, my mother gave up the apartment and moved in with Milton. She couldn't live in that apartment without me. It would be too much for her to handle.

Things continued to change.

I couldn't imagine going back up to Brooklyn and not going to my apartment. That would take some getting used to.

# SIXTEEN

It was the fourth quarter of a game against Clemson during my freshman year at Maryland. My mother was in the stands—she came down for the weekend with Milton and Gabriela—and my old teammate Leonard, a late recruit of Clemson, was on the court. It was a big game for me.

My college career had started out good. I started every game of the season, averaged fifteen points a game, and gained a reputation for being a hard-nosed defender, even though I was a freshman. NBA scouts knew who I was, and that was all I could hope for at that point in my college career. I also hadn't been late to any classes up to that point.

The game was a tight one. I was in foul trouble from the start and my time on the court was spotty. I had ten points and seven assists with two minutes left to go. The score was tied up at fifty-nine.

We came out of a timeout and Coach put the ball in my hands. I dribbled around a screen and saw an opening to drive to the hoop. But when the power forward on the other team cut off my lane, I jumped in the air to make a pass. My high school coach used to say that unless you're Magic Johnson, jumping in the air to make a pass always ends in disaster. He was once again right, as the defender from Clemson stole the ball and ignited their fast break in the other direction. They ended up getting a wide-open three and they went up sixty-two to fifty-nine. My coach called a timeout with a minute twenty-five left to go.

"What are you doing?" my coach screamed at me. "What are you doing? If you see a lane, take it! Don't be getting into the fuckin' air to make passes!"

He took a step away from me to catch his breath. His face was red and sweat was pouring off of his bald head. I didn't say anything back to him. That would just make him explode again.

He took the clipboard and marker from one of the assistants and huddled us up.

"Okay, Darnell," he said in a much, much calmer voice. "I'm coming back to you. You owe me."

He drew up a play on the board that would hopefully lead to an open three-point shot for me. None of the other guys said anything against the play call. We were a pretty tight team and I had proven myself so far as a freshman.

"Let's go, guys!" he said.

We got back on the floor and I passed the ball inbounds to our point guard, Johnny Boyd. I ran to my spot along the baseline and waited for my big guys to stack. When they did so, I ran across to the other side of the baseline and hooked around the first screen. With my defender trailing me, I continued up to the elbow behind the three-point line and ran behind another screen. I was wide open when the point guard passed the ball back to me. I caught it cleanly, set my feet, and rose up for the shot.

Splash.

The crowd went nuts. Clemson called a timeout.

The only problem was that I stepped on the three-point line, making the shot a two pointer and leaving us down one point, sixty-two to sixty-one.

Coach didn't get mad at me for that. He just patted me on the back of the head and said: "Good shot."

Fifty-five seconds were left in the game. We just had to play tough defense, get the rebound, and go down and score to win the game.

Clemson brought the ball in and was in no hurry to attack. The clock dwindled to thirty-five seconds before they started to attack. With only five seconds left on the shot clock, Clemson's best player, D'Anthony Maxwell, drove into the lane on one our best defenders, a junior named Tommy Hernandez. Maxwell got Tommy leaning with two seconds on the shot clock and before it expired, Tommy reached in and hacked Maxwell. The whole arena gasped and then moaned. Our coach went ballistic.

Two free throws for Clemson. We had no time-outs left. Twenty seconds to go.

He made the first shot right in front of our raucous cheering section; we were down two. Coach yelled out instructions for our final possession, but I couldn't hear him. I couldn't hear anything. Not the crowd. Not the other players.

Maxwell took the second free throw and it bounced in and out. Our center grabbed the rebound. The game had been a real defensive struggle right from the tip. We fought through it all night and I didn't think that we had the energy to go to overtime. If I got the ball in my hands, I was going to take a three-pointer for the win.

Brooklyn doesn't go for overtime.

I ran to the baseline as Johnny pushed the ball up the floor. I caught Johnny's eye and faked the same action from the previous possession. My defender tried to anticipate my movement and go over the screen, but I faded back into the corner instead. I made sure to set my feet behind the three-point line. Johnny hit me with a perfect pass and I was all alone in the corner. I rose up to shoot and win the game. I took that shot a million times in practice. It felt good coming off my hand. It was right online.

Front rim.

Left it an inch short.

The buzzer was the only thing I heard.

Clemson's game.

My teammates gave me pats on the back and told me to keep my head up as we walked off the court dog tired and deflated.

Coach met me in front of the bench and we walked to the locker room side by side. He put an arm around my shoulder.

"You New York kids," he said with a shake of his head. "You guys got guts."

I didn't say anything. I didn't correct him and tell him to specify that I was a Brooklyn guy, not just a New York guy.

"You got plenty of talent, D. Now I gotta get you to play smarter," he said.

"I'll get there, Coach."

"There's no doubt," he said as we walked into the locker room. "You're gonna be a player."

The door shut behind us and all the sounds of disappointment and sadness were left outside.

———

I was one of the last players out of the locker room and when I got out there, my mother, Gabriela, and Milton were there to meet me.

Gabriela ran over to hug me and finished with a little kiss on the cheek.

My mother and Milton joined us. I wrapped

my arms around my mother for the first time in months. Because I lived in Brooklyn with her my whole life, I wasn't used to waiting to give her a hug. It was something new that hurt a little at the beginning, but it was also something I'd get used to. She squeezed me tight and I leaned my head down so she could give me a kiss on the cheek.

It felt good.

"I'm so proud of you," she whispered before pulling out of the hug.

There were tears running down her face.

"Hello, Darnell," Milton said.

I shook his hand and looked him right in the eye.

"What's up Milton?" I said. "How short was my last jumper? I thought I had it."

"It looked good from here," he said.

My mother wiped her tears with a tissue and then blew her nose.

"You played a great game, and Milt is right, that

last shot looked good," my mother said, balling the tissue up and putting it in her coat pocket.

"It felt good," I said.

I was drained physically and mentally, but I didn't want to show any of the fatigue to the people I loved.

"We should probably go," I said.

"Yes, yes. Let's go get some dinner," my mother said.

"Okay," I said, putting an arm around her as we started to walk. Gabriela's sweet-smelling self was also right by my side, and Milton followed closely behind.

"Are they feeding you good here?" my mother asked. "Don't let me find out that you're down here eating crap."

"I got choices down here, Mom," I said with a smile. "Always choices."